A Midsummer Night's Dream

Translated

William Shakespeare

translated by

SJ Hills

Faithfully Translated
into Performable Modern English
Side by Side with Original Text

Includes Stage Directions

A COMEDY

Book 12 in a series of 42

This Work First Published In 2019
by DTC Publishing, London.
www.InteractiveShakespeare.com

This paperback edition first published in 2019

Typeset by DTC Publishing.

Translated from A Midsummer Night's Dream by Shakespeare, circa 1595-96.

Revised Edition. A-IV

ISBN 978-1-701-80119-6

Interactive Shakespeare
Making the past accessible

SJ Hills Writing Credits: Dramatic Works.

Shakespeare Translated Series. Modern English With Original Text.
    Faithfully translated line by line for students, actors and fans of Shakespeare.
Macbeth Translated
Romeo & Juliet Translated
Hamlet Translated
A Midsummer Night's Dream Translated
Othello Translated

Dramatised Classic Works.
    Twenty-two dramatised works written and produced by SJ Hills for
Encyclopaedia Britannica, based on classic stories including Shakespeare, for
audiences of all ages around the world.
Greatest Tales of the World. Vol 1.
Greatest Tales of the World. Vol 2.

New Works Inspired By Classic Restoration Comedy Plays.
    Scarborough Fair - inspired by *The Relapse*
    To Take A Wife - inspired by *The Country Wife*
    Wishing Well - inspired by *Epsom Wells*
    Love In A Nunnery - inspired by *The Assignation.*

Modernised English Classic Works.
    The Faerie Queene
    Beowulf
    The Virtuous Wife
    Love's Last Shift
    Wild Oats
    The Way of the World

Dedicated to my four little terrors;
Melody
Eve
James
Hamilton

"From an ardent love of literature, a profound admiration of the men who have left us legacies of thought and beauty, and, I suppose, from that feature in man that induces us to strive to follow those we most admire, and looking upon the pursuit of literature as one of the noblest in which no labour should be deemed too great, I have sought to add a few thoughts to the store already bequeathed to the world. If they are approved, I shall have gained my desire; if not, I shall hope to receive any hints in the spirit of one who loves his work and desires to progress."

R. Hilton. 1869

PREFACE

When we studied Shakespeare at school we had to flick back and forth to the notes at the back of the book to understand a confusing line, words we were not familiar with, expressions lost in time, or even current or political references of Shakespeare's time.

What if the text was rewritten to make each line clear without looking up anything?

There are plenty of modern translations just for this. But they are cumbersome to read, no flow, matter of fact translations (and most this author has found are of varying inaccuracy, despite being approved by exam boards).

As a writer and producer of drama, I wanted not only to translate the play faithfully line by line, but also to include the innuendos, the political satire, the puns and the bawdy humour in a way which would flow and bring the work to life for students, actors prepping for a performance or lovers of the work to enjoy today, faithful to the feel and meaning of the original script and language without going into lengthy explanations for a modern day audience.

A faithful line-by-line translation into modern phrasing that flows, along with additional staging directions making the play interesting to read, easy to understand, and very importantly, an invaluable study aid.

For me it all started at about eight or nine years of age. I was reading a comic which contained the story of Macbeth serialized in simple comic strip form. I could not wait to see what happened next so I rushed out to the public library to get a copy of the book. Of course, when I got it home I didn't even recognise it as being the same story. It made no sense to me, being written in 'Olde English' and often using 'flowery' language. I remember thinking at the time that one day I should write my version of the story for others to understand.

Years went by and I had pretty much forgotten my idea. Then quite by chance I was approached by Encyclopaedia Britannica to produce a series of dramatised classic dramas as educational aids for children learning English as a second language. Included in the selection was Romeo And Juliet which I was to condense down to fifty minutes using modern English.

This brought flooding back the memories of being eight years old again, reading my comic and planning my modern version of Shakespeare. In turn it also led me to the realisation that even if a reader could understand English well, this did not mean they could fully understand and enjoy Shakespeare. I could understand English, yet I did not fully understand some of Shakespeare's text without serious research. So what hope did a person whose first language was not English have?

After some investigation, I discovered there was a great desire around the world to understand the text fully without the inconvenience of referring to footnotes or sidelines, or worse still, the internet. How can one enjoy the wonderful drama with constant interruption? I was also surprised to discover the desire was equally as great in English speaking countries as ones whose first language was not English.

The final kick to get me started was meeting fans of Shakespeare's works who knew scripts off by heart but secretly admitted to me that they did have trouble fully understanding the meaning of some lines. Although they knew the storyline well they could miss some of the subtlety and innuendo Shakespeare was renowned for. It is hardly surprising in this day and age as many of the influences, trends, rumours, beliefs and current affairs of Shakespeare's time are not valid today.

I do not pretend my work is any match for the great master, but I do believe in the greater enjoyment for all. These great works deserve to be understood by all, Shakespeare himself wrote for all levels of audience, he would even aim his work to suit a particular audience at times – for example changing historical facts if he knew a member of royalty would be seeing his play and it would cause them any embarrassment, or of course to curry favour with a monarch by the use of flattery.

I have been as faithful as possible with my version, but the original, iambic pentameter, (the tempo and pace the lines were written for), and other Elizabethan tricks of the trade that Shakespeare was so brilliant at are not included unless vital to the text and meaning. For example, rhyming couplets to signify the end of a scene, for in Shakespeare's day there were no curtains, no lights and mostly static scenery, so scene changes were not so obvious, these couplets, though not strictly necessary, are included to maintain the feel of the original.

This makes for a play that sounds fresh to today's listening audience. It is also a valuable educational tool; English Literature courses often include a section on translating Shakespeare. I am often asked the meaning of a particular line, sometimes scholars argue over the meaning of particular lines. I have taken the most widely agreed version and the one which flows best with the story line where there is dispute, and if you read this translation before reading the original work or going to see a stage version, you will find the play takes on a whole new meaning, making it infinitely more enjoyable.

SJ Hills. London. 2018

Author's Note: This version contains stage directions. These are included purely as a guide to help understand the script better. Any director staging the play would have their own interpretation of the play and decide their own directions. These directions are my own personal interpretation and not those of Shakespeare. You may change these directions to your own choosing or ignore them completely. For exam purposes these should be only regarded as guidance to the dialogue and for accuracy should not be quoted in any studies or examinations.

A Midsummer Night's Dream is a comedy. Not in the same way we now know comedy, but because it focuses on the physical relationships of lovers more so than their emotional relationships and includes a happy conclusion. Farcical elements such as the transformation of one character into an ass and mistaken identity along with surreal or supernatural elements make it a light hearted romp, unlike the histories or tragedies. Other notable comedies were *The Taming Of The Shrew*, *Twelfth Night*, and *The Tempest*.

To aid in understanding speeches and for learning lines, where possible, speeches by any character are not broken over two pages unless they have a natural break. As a result of this, gaps will be noticeable at the bottom of pages where the next speech will not fully fit onto the page. This was intentional. A speech can not be fully appreciated if one has to turn the page back and forth when studying or learning lines.

Coming soon, *A Midsummer Night's Dream For All Ages* by SJ Hills, which includes the script in modern English with study note stickies, illustrations and simplified text running alongside the main text for younger readers to share with students, actors and fans of the great work.

And available soon, a wonderful, innovative app, a huge undertaking and the very first of its kind, which will include full, new interactive filmed versions of Shakespeare's plays in both original and modern English.

For further info

www.InteractiveShakespeare.com

www.facebook.com/InteractiveShakespeare

@iShakes1 on Twitter

Historical Notes

Normally, Shakespeare's sources for his plays were printed stories, plays, poems or history books, but for *A Midsummer Night's Dream*, there is no known single source for the plot. The component parts he used appear to have come from a variety of sources and from his own knowledge and imagination.

A Midsummer Night's Dream sources include *Chaucer's 'Knight's Tale'* from the *'Canterbury Tales'* which tells the story of *Theseus* conquering the Amazons and bringing *Hippolyta* home to be his queen and their subsequent wedding, with *Hippolyta's* sister performing a rite of May and *Theseus* and *Hippolyta* hunting with their hounds early on a May morning.

The story of *Pyramus* and *Thisbe* can be found in *Ovid's 'Metamorphoses'*, as well as *Chaucer's 'Legend of Good Women'*. The fairy folk were from tradition and from literature, *Edmund Spencer* calls the king of the fairies *Oberon* in his epic poem, *'Faerie Queene'* as do other sources. *Titania* can also be found in *'Metamorphoses'*, and the devilish sprite *Puck*, or *Robin Goodfellow*, was named in the ballad *'The Merry Puck, Or Robin Goodefellow'* which was known to predate this play. For the clowns, Shakespeare may simply have based them on tradesmen he knew, except for the comically named *Bottom*, who can be linked to *'St Paul's letter to the Corinthians'* in the bible for his vision, and *'The Discoverie of Witchcraft'* for transformations of humans into animals and again the troublesome sprite *Robin Goodfellow*.

Everything else probably came from the bard's own imagination and extensive knowledge of folklore. Shakespeare's use of pre-existing material was not considered a lack of originality. In Elizabethan times copyright law did not exist, copying whole passages of text was frequently practiced and not considered theft as it is today. Nowadays, stage and movie productions are frequently 'adaptations' from other sources, the only difference being the need to obtain permission or rights to do so, unless the work is out of copyright.

The real skill Shakespeare displays is in how he adapts his sources in new ways, displaying a remarkable understanding of human psyche and emotion, and including a talent at building characters, adding characters for effect, dramatic pacing, tension building, interspersed by short bouts of relief before building the tension even further, and above all of course, his extraordinary ability to use and miss-use language to his and dramatic, bawdy or playful advantage.

It has been said Shakespeare almost wrote screenplays, predating modern cinema by over 400 years, however you view it, he wrote a powerful story and understood how to play on human emotions and weaknesses.

This play was written during the reign of Elizabeth I. As Shakespeare often referred to the reigning monarch in his plays indirectly and often performed his plays before the monarch this is useful to know.

DRAMATIS PERSONAE

THESEUS,	Duke of Athens.
HIPPOLYTA,	Queen of the Amazons, betrothed to Theseus.
EGEUS,	Father to Hermia.
HERMIA,	Daughter to Egeus, in love with Lysander.
HELENA,	in love with Demetrius.
LYSANDER,	loved by Hermia
DEMETRIUS,	in love with Hermia.
PHILOSTRATE,	Theseus' Master of the Revels.

PETER QUINCE,	a Carpenter,	}
SNUG,	a Joiner,	}
NICK BOTTOM,	a Weaver,	}
FRANCIS FLUTE,	a Bellows-mender,	} Players in the Interlude.
TOM SNOUT,	a Tinker,	}
ROBIN STARVELING,	a Tailor,	}

OBERON,	King of the Fairies.
TITANIA,	Queen of the Fairies.
PUCK,	or Robin Goodfellow, a troublesome hobgoblin.

PEASEBLOSSOM,	}
COBWEB,	} Fairies
MOTH,	}
MUSTARDSEED,	}

A TRUMPETER.

Other Fairies attending on Oberon and Titania.
Lords attending on Theseus and Hippolyta.

CONTENTS

ACT I

ATHENS

AND A WOOD NEAR IT
WHERE OUR TALE IS SET

THE COURSE OF TRUE LOVE NEVER DID RUN SMOOTH

ACT I

ACT I SCENE I

ATHENS. THE PALACE OF THESEUS.

> *Note: In Greek mythology, Theseus (son of either Poseidon or Aegeus, king of Athens – stories differ) was the legendary hero of Attica,. He slew the Cretan Minotaur with the help of Ariadne, and captured Antiope, queen of the Amazons. In revenge Hippolyte invaded Attica to rescue Antiope. Theseus won and married Hippolyte, the woman he had defeated in battle.*
>
> *To show characters are comedic or to vary the overall structure of the play, Shakespeare sometimes writes lines in prose rather than the usual blank verse (a form of poetry which doesn't rhyme except for dramatic effect). He moves between prose and verse to give his characters more depth and variety by breaking the rhythm.*
>
> *Deliberate bawdy use of words is underlined, rhymed lines are in italics. Midsummer Night's Dream has the second highest percentage of rhyming lines of Shakespeare's plays at almost half of all lines.*

THE PLAY STARTS WITH THESEUS (A GRECIAN DUKE), HIPPOLYTA (HIS WIFE TO BE), PHILOSTRATE (ENTERTAINMENT MANAGER), AND ATTENDANTS.

THESEUS

Now, lovely Hippolyta, the hour of our wedding is fast approaching. In four happy days there'll be a new moon – but oh, to me how slow the old moon wanes! It delays access to my desire, like a step-mother or a widower long living out a young son's inheritance.

HIPPOLYTA

Four days will quickly plunge into night, four nights will quickly pass in dreaming, then the new crescent moon, like a silver bow newly made in heaven, shall overlook the night of our wedding ceremony.

THESEUS

Now, fair Hippolyta, our nuptial hour
Draws on apace; four happy days bring in
Another moon - but O, methinks how slow
This old moon wanes! She lingers my desires,
Like to a stepdame or a dowager
Long withering out a young man's revenue.

HIPPOLYTA

Four days will quickly steep themselves in night,
Four nights will quickly dream away the time;
And then the moon, like to a silver bow
New-bent in heaven, shall behold the night
Of our solemnities.

> *Note: The crescent moon looks like an archer's bow.*

THESEUS

Go, Philostrate, rouse the Athenian youths in merriment. Awake their young, nimble, high spirits. Divert gloom away towards funerals. Such a pale faced companion is not for our celebrations.

THESEUS

Go, Philostrate,
Stir up the Athenian youth to merriments;
Awake the pert and nimble spirit of mirth;
Turn melancholy forth to funerals.
The pale companion is not for our pomp.

EXIT PHILOSTRATE, THE ENTERTAINMENT MANAGER.

THESEUS (CONT'D)

Hippolyta, I seduced you with my sword, and won your love by defeating you in battle, but I will wed you to a different song, with splendour, with ceremony and with much celebration.

THESEUS

Hippolyta, I wooed thee with my sword,
And won thy love doing thee injuries;
But I will wed thee in another key:
With pomp, with triumph, and with revelling.

ENTER EGEUS WITH HIS DAUGHTER HERMIA, FOLLOWED BY LYSANDER, AND DEMETRIUS.

Note: Hermia and Lysander are in love. Demetrius has a crush on Hermia, but she has no feelings for him. Helena is in love with Demetrius, but he does not love her. Write this down on a piece of paper now and keep it handy. Egeus has three syllables.

EGEUS

Happiness to Theseus, our esteemed duke.

EGEUS

Happy be Theseus, our renowned duke.

THESEUS

Thank you, good Eugeus. What news about yourself?

THESEUS

Thanks, good Egeus. What's the news with thee?

EGEUS

I come full of troubles, I have problems with my child, my daughter Hermia.
(*to Demetrius*) Step forward, Demetrius.
(*to Theseus*) My noble lord, this man has my consent to marry her. (*indicates Demetrius*)
(*to Lysander*) Step forward, Lysander.
(*to Theseus*) But, my gracious Duke, this man has bewitched the heart of my child.
(*he indicates Lysander*)

EGEUS

Full of vexation come I, with complaint
Against my child, my daughter Hermia.
Stand forth, Demetrius. My noble lord,
This man hath my consent to marry her.
Stand forth, Lysander. And, my gracious duke,
This man hath bewitch'd the bosom of my child.

Note: There is one syllable too many in the last line. Early quarto texts included the word "man", but it may be that the word "man" was copied over from the line two lines above during early printing. Later folio texts omitted the word "man". It was later put back in with "bewitched" changed to "bewitch'd".

EGEUS (CONT'D)

(*to Lysander*) You, you, Lysander, you have written her poems, and swapped love tokens with my child. You have sung verses of false love with a false voice at her window by moonlight. And you've given her false impressions of love with lockets of your hair, rings, baubles, ornaments, fancy presents, knick-knacks, curiosities, perfumes, confectionary - all persuasive temptations to a young, innocent lady. With deceptive cunning you have stolen my daughter's heart, and turned her obedience, which is rightfully mine, to stubborn obstinacy.

(*to Theseus*) And, my gracious duke, if she will not here and now, before your grace, consent to marry Demetrius, I beg the time honoured privilege of Athens that, as she is mine, I may be rid of her as I please, which shall be either to this gentleman, or to her death, in accordance with the law in such a case.

EGEUS

Thou, thou, Lysander, thou hast given her rhymes,
And interchanged love-tokens with my child.
Thou hast by moonlight at her window sung,
With feigning voice, verses of feigning love;
And stol'n the impression of her fantasy
With bracelets of thy hair, rings, gauds, conceits,
Knacks, trifles, nosegays, sweetmeats - messengers
Of strong prevailment in unhardened youth.
With cunning hast thou filched my daughter's heart;
Turned her obedience, which is due to me,
To stubborn harshness. And, my gracious duke,
Be it so she will not here before your grace
Consent to marry with Demetrius,
I beg the ancient privilege of Athens:
As she is mine I may dispose of her;
Which shall be either to this gentleman
Or to her death, according to our law
Immediately provided in that case.

> Note: According to the law of Solon, parents in Athens had absolute power of life and death over their own children.
>
> In Shakespeare's time in England a daughter was considered the possession of her father until she married, then her ownership passed to her husband. Hence the father giving away the bride in the marriage ceremony. Women had no rights then.
>
> 'Bracelets of thy hair' – a common love token was a bracelet made from the giver's woven or braided hair.

THESEUS

What do you say, Hermia? Be advised, dear maiden, your father should be as a god to you. The one who gave you your beauty, yes, and the one to whom you are no more than a waxwork figure, shaped by him, and within his power to leave the figure untouched or to disfigure it. Demetrius is a worthy gentleman.

THESEUS

What say you, Hermia? Be advised fair maid.
To you your father should be as a god;
One that composed your beauties, yea, and one
To whom you are but as a form in wax
By him imprinted, and within his power
To leave the figure or disfigure it.
Demetrius is a worthy gentleman.

HERMIA

So is Lysander.

HERMIA

So is Lysander.

THESEUS
In himself he is, but in this case, lacking your father's approval, the other man must be considered more worthy.

HERMIA
I wish my father could see it with my eyes.

THESEUS
Or rather, your eyes should see with his judgement in mind.

HERMIA
I do beg your grace's pardon. I don't know by what power I am so emboldened, nor how appropriate it is to my modesty in such high presence here to plead my thoughts, but I beg that your grace tell me the worst that may befall me in this matter, if I refuse to marry Demetrius.

THESEUS
Either to die a death, or to abstain forever from the company of men. Therefore, pretty Hermia, question your desires, consider how young you are, examine fully your hot bloodedness, and whether, if you do not give in to your father's wishes, you can endure the outfit of a nun, forever to be caged in a dark cloister to live as a childless sister all your life, chanting dull hymns to the cold barren moon.

THESEUS
In himself he is;
But in this kind, wanting your father's voice,
The other must be held the worthier.

HERMIA
I would my father looked but with my eyes.

THESEUS
Rather your eyes must with his judgement look.

HERMIA
I do entreat your grace to pardon me.
I know not by what power I am made bold,
Nor how it may concern my modesty
In such a presence here to plead my thoughts;
But I beseech your grace that I may know
The worst that may befall me in this case,
If I refuse to wed Demetrius.

THESEUS
Either to die the death, or to abjure
For ever the society of men.
Therefore, fair Hermia, question your desires,
Know of your youth, examine well your blood,
Whether, if you yield not to your father's choice,
You can endure the livery of a nun,
For aye to be in shady cloister mewed,
To live a barren sister all your life,
Chanting faint hymns to the cold fruitless moon.

Note: The moon was associated with Diana, goddess of women and chastity, suggesting a sexless life with no children.

'Cloister mewed' has nothing to do with cats, it is a hawking term. Shakespeare was fond of inserting falconry references. A mew is a place or a cage where a trained hawk is placed alone to moult (mew) its feathers. From this we get the term 'mews' for a row of converted dwellings designed for stabling horses. The first mews in this sense was the Hawk Mews royal stables at Charing Cross in London.

'Cloister' – a convent, named after the arched walkways they contained. Nuns, known as sisters, were locked away in cloister where they wore rough heavy clothing which exposed only their face, and were banished to a life of prayer away from any relationships with men.

THESEUS (CONT'D)

Triple blessed are they who can forgo their passions and endure such a chaste life. But happier on earth is the rose that is picked and enjoyed, than the one withering on the virgin thorny stem, left to grow, live, and die single but blessed in heaven.

THESEUS

Thrice blessed they that master so their blood
To undergo such maiden pilgrimage;
But earthlier happy is the rose distilled
Than that which withering on the virgin thorn
Grows, lives, and dies in single blessedness.

Note: 'Blessedness' – divine blessing which comes to those who live life celibate, as nuns do.

HERMIA

And that's how I will grow, and live, and die, my lord, before I give up my virginity to his lordship, whose undesired clutches my soul does not wish to give ownership.

HERMIA

So will I grow, so live, so die, my lord,
Ere will I yield my virgin patent up
Unto his lordship, whose unwished yoke
My soul consents not to give sovereignty.

Note: 'Yoke' - the wooden bar attached to a working ox.

THESEUS

Take time to think on the matter, and by the next new moon – the day that seals the everlasting bond of fellowship between my love and I – upon that day either prepare to die for disobedience of your father's orders, or else marry Demetrius as he wishes, or on the altar of Diana, goddess of chastity, make solemn vows to austerity and a single life.

THESEUS

Take time to pause; and by the next new moon -
The sealing-day betwixt my love and me
For everlasting bond of fellowship -
Upon that day either prepare to die
For disobedience to your father's will,
Or else to wed Demetrius, as he would;
Or on Diana's altar to protest
For aye austerity and single life.

Note: 'Protest' meant to make a vow, before it meant disapproval as it does now.

'Austerity' was a clever choice of word, having three different meanings all relevant here. 1) stern/severe. ii) Plain/simple. iii) Impoverished.

Trivia: The last line is an example of a 'hendiady'. Two words connected with 'and' when they can exist together without it. 'Austerity and single life', when 'austere single life' would suffice. Shakespeare uses the 'and' to keep the iambic pentameter. (Ten alternate syllables, five short, five long).

DEMETRIUS

Give up, sweet Hermia, and, Lysander, give up your hopeless claim to my assured right.

DEMETRIUS

Relent, sweet Hermia; and, Lysander, yield
Thy crazed title to my certain right.

LYSANDER

You have her father's love, Demetrius, let me have Hermia's, you can marry him.

LYSANDER

You have her father's love, Demetrius;
Let me have Hermia's: do you marry him.

EGEUS

Sneering Lysander! It's true, he has my love,
and I shall offer him what is also mine to
love. She is mine, and all my rights of claim
to her I do bestow upon Demetrius.

LYSANDER

(*to Theseus*) I am, my lord, from as noble
descent as him and as wealthy. My love is
greater than his, my prospects in every way
of equal level, if not better than Demetrius.
And what is more than all these boasts
together, I am loved by the beautiful Hermia.
Why should I not pursue my right of claim?
I'll say it to his face, Demetrius pursued love
with Nedar's daughter, Helena, and won her
love, and she, sweet lady that she is, dotes
on him, dotes in foolish love on this immoral
and inconsistent man.

THESEUS

I must confess that I have heard the same,
and I had been meaning to speak with
Demetrius about it. But, being overrun with
personal affairs, it had slipped my mind. But,
Demetrius, come, and you, Egeus, you shall
come with me too. I have some private
words of advice for you both. As for you,
beautiful Hermia, look to ready yourself to
fit your thoughts around your father's
wishes, or else the law of Athens, which I
can in no way overturn, demands death or a
vow of chastity.

EGEUS

Scornful Lysander! True, he hath my love.
And what is mine my love shall render him;
And she is mine, and all my right of her
I do estate unto Demetrius.

LYSANDER

I am, my lord, as well derived as he,
As well possessed; my love is more than his;
My fortunes every way as fairly ranked,
If not with vantage, as Demetrius';
And, which is more than all these boasts can be,
I am beloved of beauteous Hermia.
Why should not I then prosecute my right?
Demetrius, I'll avouch it to his head,
Made love to Nedar's daughter, Helena, *Charac d*
And won her soul; and she, sweet lady, dotes, *Derivive*
Devoutly dotes, dotes in idolatry,
Upon this spotted and inconstant man.

THESEUS

I must confess that I have heard so much,
And with Demetrius thought to have spoke
  thereof;
But, being overfull of self-affairs,
My mind did lose it. But, Demetrius, come;
And come, Egeus; you shall go with me.
I have some private schooling for you both.
For you, fair Hermia, look to arm yourself
To fit your fancies to your father's will,
Or else the law of Athens yields you up -
Which by no means we may extenuate -
To death or to a vow of single life.

THESEUS STANDS TO LEAVE.

HIPPOLYTA LOOKS CONCERNED.

THESEUS (CONT'D)

Come, my dear Hippolyta. Are you all right,
my love?
- Demetrius and Egeus, come with us, I have
some tasks for you in connection with our
wedding, and I wish to discuss with you
something closely concerning you both.

THESEUS

Come, my Hippolyta; what cheer, my love?
Demetrius and Egeus, go along:
I must employ you in some business
Against our nuptial, and confer with you
Of something nearly that concerns yourselves.

EGEUS
With dutiful eagerness we follow you.

EGEUS
With duty and desire we follow you.

EXEUNT ALL BUT LYSANDER AND HERMIA.

LYSANDER NOTICES HOW UPSET HERMIA LOOKS.

LYSANDER
What now, my love! Why are your cheeks so pale? What makes the rosiness in them fade so fast?

LYSANDER
How now, my love! Why is your cheek so pale? How chance the roses there do fade so fast?

HERMIA
(sad and moody) Probably a lack of rain, which I could well provide them with from the storm in my eyes.

HERMIA
Belike for want of rain, which I could well Beteem them from the tempest of my eyes.

LYSANDER TRIES TO CONSOLE HERMIA, BUT HE IS NOT VERY GOOD AT IT.

LYSANDER
Alas, that everything I have ever read or heard told in stories or history proves that the course of true love never runs smoothly. Or it was because of a class difference...

LYSANDER
Ay me; for aught that ever I could ever read, Could ever hear by tale or history, The course of true love never did run smooth; But either it was different in blood -

Note: "The course of true love never did run smooth" - the famous quote of the play.

HERMIA IS NOT TO BE CONSOLED. SHE LOVES LYSANDER BUT MUST MARRY DEMETRIUS.

HERMIA
(interrupting) What a cross to bear! Too high class to be in love with a commoner.

HERMIA
O cross! - too high to be enthralled to low.

Note: 'Cross' – the cross Jesus was crucified on, which he had to carry to the site of the crucifixion. "A cross to bear" is a saying still in use today, meaning a burden or trial that has to be endured.

LYSANDER
Or there was a mismatch in age...

LYSANDER
Or else misgraffed in respect of years -

HERMIA
(interrupting) So unfair! Too old to be engaged to a young one.

HERMIA
O spite! - too old to be engaged to young.

22

LYSANDER
Or else it was down to the choice of your friends and relatives...

HERMIA
(*interrupting*) Oh hell! To choose love through another's eyes!

LYSANDER
Or, even if all parties were happy with the choice, then war, death, or sickness could confound it, making it as short lived as a sound, swift as a shadow, fleeting as a dream, brief as the lightning in the black night which, in a fit of anger, reveals both heaven and earth, and before a man has time to say 'look!' the jaws of darkness have devoured it. That's how quickly bright hopes can be destroyed.

LYSANDER
Or else it stood upon the choice of friends -

HERMIA
O hell! - to choose love by another's eyes.

LYSANDER
Or, if there were a sympathy in choice,
War, death, or sickness did lay siege to it,
Making it momentary as a sound,
Swift as a shadow, short as any dream,
Brief as the lightning in the collied night
That, in a spleen, unfolds both heaven and
 earth,
And ere a man hath power to say `Behold!'
The jaws of darkness do devour it up.
So quick bright things come to confusion.

Note: 'Spleen' – used in the context of 'venting his spleen'. It was once believed that the spleen was the source of a bad temper.

'Confusion' – Shakespeare often uses the word to mean 'ruin'.

HERMIA
Then if true lovers have always been thwarted, it must be a rule of fate. In which case, let us learn patience at such trials, because it is an expected cross to bear, as much a part of love as thoughts and dreams and sighs, hopes and tears, love's poor companions.

HERMIA
If then true lovers have been ever crossed,
It stands as an edict in destiny.
Then let us teach our trial patience,
Because it is a customary cross,
As due to love as thoughts and dreams and sighs,
Wishes and tears, poor fancy's followers.

Note: 'Cross' – the heavy wooden cross Christ had to carry to be crucified on.

LYSANDER

A good outlook. Therefore, hear me out, Hermia. I have a widowed aunt, with an inheritance of great income. She is childless and she regards me as her only son. Her house is twenty miles away from Athens, and there, sweet Hermia, I can marry you, out of the jurisdiction of cruel Athenian law. If you love me, slip out of your father's house tomorrow night, and in the wood three miles outside town, where I met you and Helena to perform May Day rites one morning, I will be waiting for you there.

LYSANDER

A good persuasion. Therefore hear me, Hermia:
I have a widow aunt, a dowager
Of great revenue, and she hath no child -
From Athens is her house remote seven leagues -
And she respects me as her only son.
There, gentle Hermia, may I marry thee,
And to that place the sharp Athenian law
Cannot pursue us. If thou lov'st me then,
Steal forth thy father's house tomorrow night,
And in the wood, a league without the town,
Where I did meet thee once with Helena
To do observance to a morn of May,
There will I stay for thee.

Note: A league is roughly three miles or five kilometres. Twenty miles is roughly thirty-two kilometres.

May Day rites are performed early on the first day of May. They celebrate the oncoming spring and are performed to bring on a good harvest.

HERMIA

My dear Lysander, I swear to you by Cupid's strongest bow, by his best gold tipped arrow,
By the innocence of Venus' doves,
By that which unites souls and furthers loves,
And by the fire which burned the Carthage queen,
When the false Trojan under sail was seen.
By all the vows that men have ever broke –
In number more than women ever spoke –
In that same place you have instructed me,
Tomorrow truly I will meet with thee.

HERMIA

My good Lysander,
I swear to thee by Cupid's strongest bow,
By his best arrow with the golden head,
By the simplicity of Venus' doves,
By that which knitteth souls and prospers loves,
And by that fire which burned the Carthage queen
When the false Trojan under sail was seen;
By all the vows that ever men have broke -
In number more than ever women spoke -
In that same place thou hast appointed me,
Tomorrow truly I will meet with thee.

Note: In Ovid's 'Metamorphoses', Cupid's gold tipped arrow created lovers, his lead tipped one had the opposite effect.

Aphrodite and Venus, the goddesses of love, were depicted with sweet doves flying around them or perched on them.

The 'Carthage queen' was Dido who fell in love with Aeneas (the false Trojan). She stabbed herself and was burned on a pyre when he deserted her by sailing away.

Trivia: In the case of Venus' dropping the extra 's, i.e. Venus's, the extra 's is dropped for classical names but not ordinary names. Tennis player Venus's tennis serve, is correct for example, but not for the Venus of mythology. It is pronounced 'venus-ses' in both cases.

Act I Scene I - Athens. The Palace of Theseus.

LYSANDER
Keep your promise, my love. Look, here comes Helena.

LYSANDER
Keep promise, love. Look, here comes Helena.

ENTER HELENA IN A HURRY.

HERMIA
God speed, fair Helena! Going away?

HERMIA
God speed, fair Helena! Whither away?

Note: For the wordplay on 'fair', consider its meaning as 'beauty' or 'beautiful'.

HELENA
You call me fair? That 'fair' you must unsay.
Demetrius loves your fair – Oh, happy fair!
Your eyes are magnets, and your tongue's sweet air
More tuneful than the lark's to shepherd's ear
When wheat is green and Hawthorn buds appear.
Sickness is catching, oh, that looks were too,
Yours I'd catch, fair Hermia, to be like you!
My ear would catch your voice, my eye your eye,
My tongue would catch your tongue's sweet melody.
If the world were mine, Demetrius excepted,
The rest I'd give to be you incarnated.
Oh, teach me how you look, and with what art,
You capture the beat of Demetrius' heart.

HELENA
Call you me fair? That `fair' again unsay.
Demetrius loves your fair - O happy fair!
Your eyes are lodestars, and your tongue's sweet air
More tuneable than lark to shepherd's ear
When wheat is green, when Hawthorn buds appear.
Sickness is catching; O, were favour so,
Yours would I catch, fair Hermia, ere I go!
My ear should catch your voice, my eye your eye,
My tongue should catch your tongue's sweet melody.
Were the world mine, Demetrius being bated,
The rest I'd give to be to you translated.
O, teach me how you look, and with what art
You sway the motion of Demetrius' heart.

Note: The lark was the herald of the morning, the first bird to sing at dawn. In Romeo and Juliet it sadly announced the parting of the lovers.

Shakespeare often rhymes 'love' with 'move' or 'prove', and here he rhymes 'eye' with 'melody' – words which don't rhyme when spoken in modern English. The vowel sounds have changed over the centuries, and regional variations are very marked, add to that the poetic pronunciation of some words and it all gets lost today. For a more detailed explanation see the note on page 71.

HERMIA
I frown upon him, yet he loves me still.

HELENA
Oh, that your frowns could teach my smiles such skill.

HERMIA
I give him curses, yet he gives me love.

HELENA
Oh, that my prayers could such affection move.

HERMIA
I frown upon him, yet he loves me still.

HELENA
O that your frowns would teach my smiles such skill.

HERMIA
I give him curses, yet he gives me love.

HELENA
O that my prayers could such affection move.

25

HERMIA
The more I hate, the more he does chase me.

HELENA
The more I love, the more he does hate me.

HERMIA
His folly, Helena, is no fault of mine.

HELENA
Only your beauty – wish that fault was mine!

HERMIA
Take comfort, he shall no more see my face.
Lysander and myself will flee this place.
Before the day Lysander and I met,
Athens it seemed was in paradise set.
Oh then, what power in my love does dwell,
That has turned this heaven into a hell?

LYSANDER
Helen, to you our plans we won't conceal.
Tomorrow night, when the moon does reveal
Its silvery face in the wat'ry glass,
Coating with liquid pearls the blades of grass –
A time lovers' flight is hid from the eye –
Through Athens' gates we are planning to fly.

HERMIA
And in the wood where often you and I
Upon pale primrose beds would go to lie,
To share our problems with company sweet,
There my Lysander and myself will meet.
Away from Athens we'll avert our eye
To seek new friendships in new company.
Farewell, sweet playfellow. Do pray for us.
And good luck to you and Demetrius.
(to Lysander)
Be true, Lysander, we must starve our sight
Till we see each other, tomorrow midnight.

LYSANDER
I will, my Hermia.

HERMIA
The more I hate, the more he follows me.

HELENA
The more I love, the more he hateth me.

HERMIA
His folly, Helena, is no fault of mine.

HELENA
None but your beauty - would that fault were mine!

HERMIA
Take comfort: he no more shall see my face.
Lysander and myself will fly this place.
Before the time I did Lysander see,
Seemed Athens as a paradise to me.
O then, what graces in my love do dwell,
That he hath turned a heaven unto a hell?

LYSANDER
Helen, to you our minds we will unfold.
Tomorrow night, when Phoebe doth behold
Her silver visage in the wat'ry glass,
Decking with liquid pearl the bladed grass -
A time that lovers' flights doth still conceal -
Through Athens' gates have we devised to steal.

HERMIA
And in the wood where often you and I
Upon faint primrose-beds were wont to lie,
Emptying our bosoms of their counsel sweet,
There my Lysander and myself shall meet;
And thence from Athens turn away our eyes
To seek new friends and stranger companies.
Farewell, sweet playfellow. Pray thou for us;
And good luck grant thee thy Demetrius.

Keep word, Lysander: we must starve our sight
From lovers' food till morrow deep midnight.

LYSANDER
I will, my Hermia.

EXIT HERMIA.

LYSANDER (CONT'D)	LYSANDER
Helena, adieu.	*Helena, adieu.*
As you do him, may Demetrius love you!	*As you on him, Demetrius dote on you!*

EXIT LYSANDER, LEAVING ONLY HELENA.

HELENA	HELENA
How much happier some others can be!	*How happy some o'er other some can be!*
Through Athens I'm thought of as fair as she.	*Through Athens I am thought as fair as she.*
But so what? Demetrius does not think so.	*But what of that? Demetrius thinks not so;*
He will not accept what all but him know.	*He will not know what all but he do know;*
And just as he's wrong, loving Hermia's eyes,	*And as he errs, doting on Hermia's eyes,*
Then so am I, liking his qualities.	*So I, admiring of his qualities.*
Things gross and vile, holding no quality,	*Things base and vile, holding no quantity,*
Love can transpose in looks and dignity.	*Love can transpose to form and dignity.*
Love looks not with the eyes, but with the mind,	*Love looks not with the eyes, but with the mind,*
That is why Cupid is always shown blind.	*And therefore is winged Cupid painted blind.*
And Cupid's mind has no judgement or taste.	*Nor hath Love's mind of any judgement taste;*
Wings and no eyes suggest unheeded haste,	*Wings and no eyes figure unheedy haste;*
Hence, 'Cupid's a child', has often been said,	*And therefore is Love said to be a child,*
'Cause in his choice he is so oft misled.	*Because in choice he is so oft beguiled.*
Like rogue boys in sport who do falsely swear,	*As waggish boys in game themselves forswear,*
The young boy, Cupid, is tricked everywhere.	*So the boy Love is perjured everywhere;*
Before Demetrius spotted Hermia's eyne,	*For ere Demetrius looked on Hermia's eyne,*
He hailed down oaths that he was solely mine.	*He hailed down oaths that he was only mine;*
But then when this hail, Hermia's heat it felt,	*And when this hail some heat from Hermia felt,*
It thawed and all the showers of oaths did melt.	*So he dissolved, and showers of oaths did melt.*
I will go tell him of fair Hermia's flight.	*I will go tell him of fair Hermia's flight.*
Then to the wood he'll go tomorrow night.	*Then to the wood will he tomorrow night*
He'll find her, and for this intelligence	*Pursue her; and for this intelligence*
If he thanks me, it'll be grudging expense.	*If I have thanks, it is a dear expense.*
Though by these means I will increase my pain,	*But herein mean I to enrich my pain,*
We will at least see each other again.	*To have his sight thither and back again.*

> Note: 'Eyne' – an obsolete word for the plural of eye (eyes). Used now only in poetry,
> hence it being included in the translation for the rhyme with 'mine'.

ACT I SCENE II

ATHENS. A ROOM IN QUINCE'S HOUSE.

ENTER QUINCE THE CARPENTER, SNUG THE JOINER, BOTTOM THE WEAVER,
FLUTE THE BELLOWS MENDER, SNOUT THE TINKER (TRAVELLING METAL
REPAIRER) AND STARVELING THE TAILOR. NONE OF THEM ARE VERY BRIGHT.
THEY ARE COMMONLY REFERRED TO AS CLOWNS OR COMEDIANS.

*Note: This 'company of actors' are all tradesmen and of limited
education. The scene is possibly related to 'The Ship of Fools' from
Plato's 'Republic', where the captain has poor hearing, poor sight, and
poor navigational skills. The crew rebel, all insisting they should steer
the ship, though none of them are trained. They remove the captain
and any dissenters and, after breaking open the stores of drink and
food, fight to steer the ship with obvious disastrous and tragically
comedic consequences. In this scene, Quince has been appointed the
director, though he has no experience, and Bottom, who also has no
experience but plenty of self-confidence, wants to take over every role
in the company.*

QUINCE	QUINCE
Is all our company here?	Is all our company here?
BOTTOM	BOTTOM
You'd best call them out *generally,* (individually) *man* by *man* (one by one) from the *scrip* (script).	You were best to call them generally, man by man, according to the scrip.

*Note: 'Scrip' - Bottom means 'script'. This group of men often get words slightly
wrong, or use words that sound like the one they should have used, but have a
completely different meaning. Words they get wrong will be italicised and the correct
word will be shown next to it. Miswording here is known as a 'blunder'.*

The groups of actors of the time were known collectively as 'playing companies'.

HE INDICATES THE PAPER QUINCE IS HOLDING.

QUINCE	QUINCE
Here is the list of every man's name from all of Athens *which* (who) is thought fit to play in our *interlude* in front of the duke and the duchess on the night of their wedding day.	Here is the scroll of every man's name which is thought fit, through all Athens, to play in our interlude before the duke and the duchess on his wedding day at night

Note: An interlude is typically a pause in the middle of a play, not the play itself.

BOTTOM

First, good Peter Quince, say what the play *treats* (treads) on, then read the names of the actors to *grow to your point*. (get to the point)

QUINCE

Indeed, our play is 'The Most Lamentable *Comedy* (tragedy) And Most Cruel Death Of Pyramus And Thisbe'.

BOTTOM

First, good Peter Quince, say what the play treats on; then read the names of the actors; and so grow to a point.

QUINCE

C ay maron

Marry, our play is ' The most Lamentable Comedy and most Cruel Death of Pyramus and Thisbe'.

> Note: The play is of course a tragedy, not a comedy, though the speech is comedic.
>
> Literary Note: In mythology, Thisbe, a beautiful young Babylonian woman, was loved by Pyramus. Their parents objected to them marrying so the lovers had to meet secretly. One day they agreed to meet at the tomb of Ninus. Thisbe arrived first and saw a lioness which had just killed an ox, so she ran away. As she ran she dropped an item of clothing which the lion seized and stained with blood. Pyramus found it and thinking Thisbe had been killed, he killed himself. Thisbe, on returning to the spot, found Pyramus' dead body and killed herself.
>
> Their story is from Ovid's 'Metamorphoses' and bears some resemblance to Romeo and Juliet.

BOTTOM

A very fine piece of work, I assure you, and a *merry*. Now, good Peter Quince, call out your actors *by* (from) the list. Men, *spread yourselves*. (line up).

BOTTOM

A very good piece of work, I assure you, and a merry. Now, good Peter Quince, call forth your actors by the scroll. Masters, spread yourselves.

> Note: A merry – this doesn't make proper sense, he probably means, entertaining, or a comedy, or even a merry one, which of course it isn't, it is a tragic tale.

QUINCE

Answer as I call you.

(*calls*) Nick Bottom, the weaver?

QUINCE

Answer as I call you. Nick Bottom, the weaver?

BOTTOM

Ready. Name the part I'm down for, then proceed.

BOTTOM

Ready. Name what part I am for, and proceed.

QUINCE

You, Nick Bottom, are *set* (put) down for Pyramus.

QUINCE

You, Nick Bottom, are set down for Pyramus.

BOTTOM

What is Pyramus? A lover or a *tyrant*? (hero)

BOTTOM

What is Pyramus? A lover, or a tyrant?

QUINCE

A lover, who kills himself most *gallant* (gallantly) for love.

BOTTOM

That will cause tears if performed properly. If I do it, let the audience look out for their eyes. I will make storms of tears, I will *condole* (be sympathetic) with the character *in some measure* (in depth). Now list the others.

QUINCE

A lover, that kills himself most gallant for love.

Character? [handwritten note]

BOTTOM

That will ask some tears in true performing of it. If I do it, let the audience look to their eyes. I will move storms; I will condole in some measure. To the rest.

BOTTOM CONTINUES, NOT ALLOWING QUINCE TO LIST THE OTHERS.

BOTTOM (CONT'D)

– Yet my real passion is playing a *tyrant* (hero). I could play *Ercles* (Hercules) *rarely* (very well), or someone who rants and rages and upsets everyone.

BOTTOM

- Yet my chief humour is for a tyrant. I could play Ercles rarely, or a part to tear a cat in, to make all split.

> Note: Hercules kills a lion in his twelve labours and famously goes into a mad rage killing all his family in the Roman tragedy by Seneca, 'Hercules Furens' (The Mad Hercules).
>
> 'Tear a cat' – to rant loudly. 'Make all split' – Cause a stir amongst everyone.

HE DEMONSTRATES, RECITING VERSE IN A THEATRICAL RAGE.

BOTTOM (CONT'D)

The raging rocks
And shivering shocks
Shall break the locks
Of prison gates;
And Phibbus' car
Shall shine from afar,
And make and mar
The foolish Fates.

BOTTOM

The raging rocks
And shivering shocks
Shall break the locks
Of prison gates;
And Phibbus' car
Shall shine from far,
And make and mar
The foolish Fates.

> Note: Bottom says this rhyme is 'lofty'. Whatever it is it makes almost no sense.
>
> "Phibbus' car" – the chariot of the sun god Phoebus, which drove the sun around the earth daily.
>
> The 'Fates' were three goddesses who determined a human's destiny, or fate, as we also call it. One spun (made) the thread of life, one decided its length, and one cut it.

BOTTOM (CONT'D)

(*about his theatrical performance*) That was *lofty* (high-brow) stuff.

(*to Quince*) Now name the rest of the players.

(*again about his performance*) - That was in *Ercles* (Hercules) style, that of a *tyrant* (hero), a lover would be more *condoling*. (pathetic)

QUINCE
Francis Flute, the bellows mender?

FLUTE
Here, Peter Quince.

QUINCE
Flute, you must *take on* Thisbe.

FLUTE
What is Thisbe? – A wandering knight?

BOTTOM
This was lofty. Now name the rest of the players.
- This is Ercles' vein, a tyrant's vein; a lover is more condoling.

QUINCE
Francis Flute, the bellows-mender?

FLUTE
Here, Peter Quince.

QUINCE
Flute, you must take Thisbe on you.

FLUTE
What is Thisbe? - a wand'ring knight?

Note: Quince means play the part of Thisbe, Flute assumes it is 'take on in a fight'.

QUINCE
She is the lady that Pyramus must love.

FLUTE
No, indeed, don't let me play a woman. I'm growing a beard.

QUINCE
It is the lady that Pyramus must love.

FLUTE
Nay, faith, let me not play a woman; I have a beard coming.

Note: In Shakespeare's times, young men played the female parts in a play. It was illegal for women to act.

QUINCE
That doesn't matter, you can wear a mask, and you can speak as small (in as tiny a voice) as you wish.

BOTTOM
If I hide my face, let me play Thisbe too. I'll speak in a monstrous little (extremely small) voice.

QUINCE
That's all one. You shall play it in a mask, and you may speak as small as you will.

BOTTOM
An I may hide my face, let me play Thisbe too. I'll speak in a monstrous little voice:

HE DEMONSTRATES USING A LOUD LOW VOICE AND THEN A HIGH SQUEAKY VOICE DELIBERATELY MISPRONOUNCING THISBE'S NAME WITH A FALSE LISP.

BOTTOM (CONT'D)
(*male voice*) 'Thisne, Thisne!'
(*poor female high pitched voice*) 'Ah,
Pyramus, my lover dear. I am your dear
Thisbe, and dear lady!'

BOTTOM
` Thisne, Thisne!'
` Ah, Pyramus, my lover dear; thy Thisbe dear, and
lady dear!'

> Note: There are several theories put forward as to why Bottom should pronounce the
> name 'Thisne' when playing a hero. From being a pet name for his love, to showing
> how he would mix up his words from one character to the next, to playing a buffoon
> type character, or possibly it was a dig at another heroic actor who spoke badly.

QUINCE
No, no. You must play Pyramus - and
Flute, you will play Thisbe.

QUINCE
No, no; you must play Pyramus; and Flute, you
Thisbe.

BOTTOM
Very well, proceed.

BOTTOM
Well, proceed.

QUINCE
(*calls*) Robin Starveling, the tailor?

QUINCE
Robin Starveling, the tailor?

STARVELING
Here, Peter Quince.

STARVELING
Here, Peter Quince.

QUINCE
Robin Starveling, you must play Thisbe's
mother.
(*calls*) Tom Snout, the tinker?

QUINCE
Robin Starveling, you must play Thisbe's mother.
Tom Snout, the tinker?

SNOUT
Here, Peter Quince.

SNOUT
Here, Peter Quince.

QUINCE
You will play Pyramus' father. I myself
shall play Thisbe's father.
- Snug, the joiner, you will play the lion.
And I hope that is the play filled (fully cast).

QUINCE
You, Pyramus' father. Myself, Thisbe's father. Snug,
the joiner, you the lion's part. And I hope here is
a play fitted.

> Note: Quince has cast the father and mother of Thisbe and the father of Pyramus,
> though they do not appear in the play. Later additional characters are added, the
> Moon played by Starveling, and a Wall played by Snout.

SNUG
Have you the lion's part written down?
Please, if you do, give it me, I am slow of
learning.

SNUG
Have you the lion's part written? Pray you, if it be,
give it me, for I am slow of study.

32

QUINCE	**QUINCE**
You may make it up as you go, it is only roaring.	You may do it extempore, for it is nothing but roaring.
BOTTOM	**BOTTOM**
Let me play the lion too. My roar will make any man's heart glad to hear me. My roar will make the duke say 'Let him roar again, let him roar again.'	Let me play the lion too. I will roar that I will do any man's heart good to hear me. I will roar that I will make the duke say ˙ Let him roar again, let him roar again.'
QUINCE	**QUINCE**
If you should do it too *terribly* (terrifyingly), you would frighten the duchess and the ladies so they would scream, and that would be enough to hang us all.	An you should do it too terribly, you would fright the duchess and the ladies that they would shriek; and that were enough to hang us all.
ALL	**ALL**
That would hang us, every mother's son.	That would hang us, every mother's son.
BOTTOM	**BOTTOM**
I grant you, friends, if you frighten the ladies out of their wits they would have no discretion (hesitation) in hanging us, but I will *aggravate* (tone down) my voice so my roar will be as gentle as any *suckling dove* (cooing dove). I will roar you as if it were a nightingale.	I grant you, friends, if you should fright the ladies out of their wits they would have no more discretion but to hang us; but I will aggravate my voice so that I will roar you as gently as any sucking dove; I will roar you an 'twere any nightingale.

> Note: A dove doesn't suckle. Bottom probably confused suckling pig, and obviously a nightingale is famed for singing, not roaring.

QUINCE	**QUINCE**
You can play no part but Pyramus, for Pyramus is a sweet-faced man, a proper man, as any you'll see *in a* (on a) summer's day. A most lovely, gentlemanlike man. Therefore you *must needs* play Pyramus.	You can play no part but Pyramus; for Pyramus is a sweet-faced man; a proper man, as one shall see in a summer's day; a most lovely, gentlemanlike man. Therefore you must needs play Pyramus.

> Note: 'Must needs' – either word on its own would suffice. i.e. 'must play' or 'need to play'.

BOTTOM	**BOTTOM**
Well, I will undertake it. What beard is it best to play it in?	Well, I will undertake it. What beard were I best to play it in?
QUINCE	**QUINCE**
Why, any you like.	Why, what you will.

BOTTOM

I will *discharge* (perform) it in either a straw coloured beard, an orangey-brown beard, a purple-reddish beard, or a French crown coloured beard – a perfect yellow.

BOTTOM

I will discharge it in either your straw-colour beard, your orange-tawny beard, your purple-in-grain beard, or your French-crown-colour beard, your perfect yellow.

> Note: 'Grain' – cochineal, a red dye from the dried bodies of insects.
>
> 'Crown' - gold coin. In the next speech Quince means 'head' when he says 'crown', an old word for head, as in the rhyme, 'Jack fell down and broke his crown'. It also says that French crowns (heads) have no hair – this was because the pox (syphilis), also know as 'the French disease', caused hair loss.

QUINCE

Some of your French crowns have no hair at all, and then you will play clean shaven. But, men, here are your parts, (*he hands the scripts out*) and I am to beg you, plead with you, and desire you to learn them by tomorrow night, and meet me in the moonlit palace wood a mile outside town. There we will rehearse, for if we meet in the city we shall be dogged with company, and our plans will be known. In the meantime I will draw up a list of props that our play wants. I beg you, do not fail me.

QUINCE

Some of your French crowns have no hair at all, and then you will play barefaced. But, masters, *[handwritten: pri(ate/) shouts]* here are your parts; and I am to entreat you, request you, and desire you to con them by tomorrow night, and meet me in the palace wood a mile without the town by moonlight. There will we rehearse, for if we meet in the city we shall be dogged with company, and our devices known. In the meantime I will draw a bill of properties such as our play wants. I pray you, fail me not.

BOTTOM

We will meet, and there we can rehearse most *obscenely* (seemly) and *courageously*. (earnestly) Working hard to be word perfect. Adieu.

BOTTOM

We will meet; and there we may rehearse most obscenely and courageously. Take pains; be perfect. Adieu.

QUINCE

We'll meet at the duke's oak tree.

QUINCE

At the duke's oak we meet.

BOTTOM

That's it then.
(*to all*) Be there, no excuses.

BOTTOM

Enough; hold or cut bow-strings.

[handwritten: 10 of then will be in the woods]

> Note: There are many arguments among scholars regarding the meaning of the above line. Some say it was a common saying from archery – a man either holds the archery bow or he cuts the bow-strings for it. Others say it is about violin bows. Others that 'hold' means keep your promise or we'll cut your violin bow-strings. Whatever the source, the meaning is - be there whatever happens.

EXEUNT.

Note: Shakespeare often uses rhyming couplets to signify the end of a scene. In Shakespeare's day there were no curtains, no lights and mostly static scenery, so scene changes were not so obvious. Audiences were conditioned to hear the rhyme and knew the significance. The remainder of the play would be mostly written in blank verse, which is unrhymed, so the contrast was apparent.

However, in this play, half of the lines are rhymed so the significance is not so obvious. Often characters rhyme their last two lines as they are due to exit the stage mid scene. The rhyming lines, though not strictly necessary, are included to maintain the feel of the original.

Shakespeare also used rhyme for certain characters, and the type of rhyme (the meter, or how many syllables there are per line) would vary depending on the character who spoke it.

Important Note: The stage directions (between main text in capital letters) are included purely as the author's guide to understand the script better. Any director staging the play would have their own interpretation of the play and decide their own directions. These directions are not those of Shakespeare. You can change these directions to your own choosing or ignore them completely. For exam purposes these should only be regarded as guidance to the dialogue and for accuracy should not be quoted in any studies or examinations.

ACT II

A WOOD NEAR ATHENS

AND WITH THE JUICE OF THIS I'LL STREAK HER EYES
AND MAKE HER FULL OF HATEFUL FANTASIES

ACT II

ACT II SCENE I

A WOOD NEAR ATHENS.

ENTER FAIRY AT ONE SIDE, AND PUCK (ROBIN GOODFELLOW) AT THE OTHER.
PUCK IS A GOBLIN, A MISCHIEVOUS SPRITE, A SUPERNATURAL BEING.

PUCK
What are you up to, fairy! Where are you headed?

FAIRY
Over hill, over dale,
  Through bush, through briar,
Over park, over vale,
  Through flood, through fire.
I do wander everywhere,
Swifter than the lunar sphere.
And I serve the Fairy Queen,
Her rings I dew upon the green.
The tall cowslips, her bodyguards be,
In their gold coats, spots you'll see.
These are rubies, fairy tokens of love
In those dots sweet scent does live.
I must go seek some dewdrops here,
And hang a pearl in every cowslip's ear.
Farewell, you dolt of spirits, I'll be gone.
Our queen and all her elves will come here soon.

PUCK
How now, spirit! Whither wander you?

FAIRY
Over hill, over dale,
  Thorough bush, thorough briar,
Over park, over pale,
  Thorough flood, thorough fire.
I do wander everywhere,
Swifter than the moon's sphere;
And I serve the Fairy Queen,
To dew her orbs upon the green.
The cowslips tall her pensioners be;
In their gold coats spots you see;
Those be rubies, fairy favours;
In those freckles live their savours.
I must go seek some dewdrops here,
And hang a pearl in every cowslip's ear.
Farewell, thou lob of spirits; I'll be gone.
Our queen and all her elves come here anon.

Note: 'Pale' – fence post. He is saying fences are no barrier to him.

'Moon's sphere' – Thanks to Ptolemy, people then believed the seven visible planets (which included the Moon and the Sun) were carried around the Earth in invisible spheres, with an outer eighth sphere containing the seven planet spheres and all the stars (the firmament). The whole system was contained in a ninth sphere, the Primum Mobile, itself contained within the Empyrean, the fastest moving sphere, revolving around the earth (the centre of the system) in twenty-four hours, carrying the inner spheres with it. Shakespeare frequently mentions the spheres. Copernicus had proved by 1543 that the earth revolved around the Sun, but the Church considered this heresy.

PUCK

The fairy king will revel here tonight.
Take care the queen comes not within his
  sight,
For Oberon is full of ire and wrath
Because the queen as her attendant hath
A nice boy stolen from an Indian king.
She never had so sweet a changeling.
And jealous Oberon would like the child
To follow him wond'ring the forests wild.
But she by force keeps close the loved boy,
Crowns him with flowers, and makes him her
  joy.
And now if they should meet in grove or green,
By fountain clear, or by the starlight's sheen,
They quarrel, so that all their elves from fright
Creep into acorn cups, hidden from sight.

PUCK

The king doth keep his revels here tonight.
Take heed the queen come not within his sight,
For Oberon is passing fell and wrath,
Because that she as her attendant hath
A lovely boy, stol'n from an Indian king.
She never had so sweet a changeling;
And jealous Oberon would have the child
Knight of his train, to trace the forests wild;
But she perforce withholds the loved boy,
Crowns him with flowers, and makes him all her joy.
And now they never meet in grove or green,
By fountain clear, or spangled starlight sheen,
But they do square, that all their elves for fear
Creep into acorn cups and hide them there.

Note: 'Changeling' – a child stolen by fairies and replaced with another. Typically in folk tales a beautiful child is taken leaving an ugly one in its place.

FAIRY

Either I mistake your shape and your features,
Or you are that cunning rogue of creatures
Called Robin Goodfellow. Have you not made
The village maidens scared and afraid?
You steal the cream, and grind unwanted
  corn,
You fruitlessly make the tired housewife
  churn,
And sometimes kill dead the froth on the beer,
At night mislead walkers and laugh at their
  fear?
Some call you 'Hobgoblin', others 'Sweet
  Puck',
When you do their work, then that's their
  good luck.
Are you not he?

FAIRY

Either I mistake your shape and making quite,
Or else you are that shrewd and knavish sprite
Called Robin Goodfellow. Are not you he
That frights the maidens of the villagery,
Skim milk, and sometimes labour in the quern,
And bootless make the breathless housewife churn,
And sometimes make the drink to bear no barm,
Mislead night-wanderers, laughing at their harm?
Those that `Hobgoblin' call you, and `Sweet Puck',
You do their work, and they shall have good luck.
Are not you he?

Note: Robin Goodfellow traditionally was a domestic imp who would help servants with housework or would play mischievous tricks.

PUCK

You are quite right.
I am that merry wanderer of the night.
I joke with Oberon and do him amuse
When a horse full of beans I do confuse,
By neighing to sound like a female foal.
And sometimes I lurk in an old crone's bowl
Much looking like a beer roasted apple,
And when she drinks, her lips I do grapple,
And on her down-hanging chest spills the ale.
The old woman who tells the fireside tale,
For a three legged stool oft mistakes me.
Then I slip from her bum, and down falls she,
And 'sailor swears', as she's starting to cough.
And those gathered round hold their sides and laugh,
So taken by their mirth, they wheeze and swear
A merrier time was never enjoyed there.
But stand back, fairy! Here comes Oberon.

FAIRY

And here's my mistress. I wish he were gone!

PUCK

Thou speak'st aright;
I am that merry wanderer of the night.
I jest to Oberon, and make him smile
When I a fat and bean-fed horse beguile,
Neighing in likeness of a filly foal;
And sometime lurk I in a gossip's bowl
In very likeness of a roasted crab,
And when she drinks, against her lips I bob,
And on her withered dewlap pour the ale.
The wisest aunt, telling the saddest tale,
Sometime for three-foot stool mistaketh me;
Then slip I from her bum. Down topples she,
And `tailor' cries, and falls into a cough;
And then the whole quire hold their hips and laugh,
And waxen in their mirth, and neeze, and swear
A merrier hour was never wasted there.
But room, fairy! Here comes Oberon.

FAIRY

And here my mistress. Would that he were gone!

Note: 'Withered dewlap' is the down-hanging neck skin of cattle which 'laps' up the dew as the cattle eat grass. Shakespeare is referring to spilling the beer on an equally down-hanging chest of an old crone. She would have difficulty spilling it on her neck as most editions suggest using literal translation, whereas Shakespeare was more likely suggesting saggy breasts and his audience would assume this.

'Tailor cries' – some editions claim this is meant to be the crone sitting cross-legged on the floor like a tailor, and crying, which is solely because Johnson wrote in explanation, "He that slips beside his chair, falls as a tailor squats upon his board". It is more likely to be an expression based on trade such as 'swear like a sailor or a trooper". A 'regular tailor' was an expression meaning 'clumsy person', and as the word is highlighted in the script it is suggesting its usage was not literal, i.e. an expression rather than a literal tailor.

'Neeze' is sneeze, but sneezing with mirth is not a known old expression, so wheeze has been used in the translation as it fits the meaning better.

ENTER THE KING OF THE FAIRIES (OBERON), AT ONE DOOR, WITH HIS FAIRIES, AND THE QUEEN OF THE FAIRIES (TITANIA), AT ANOTHER, WITH HERS.

OBERON

Not happily met by moonlight, stubborn Titania.

OBERON

Ill met by moonlight, proud Titania.

TITANIA

(*suddenly noticing him*) Why, it's jealous Oberon! Fairies let's skip away. I have sworn to avoid his bed and his company.

OBERON

Wait a moment, rash, immoral woman. Am I not your husband?

TITANIA

Then I should be your wife. But I know that when you have stolen away from fairyland you take on the shape of Corin and sit all day playing on corn pipes, and reciting love poems to the seductress, Phillida. What brings you here, all the way from the farthest reaches of India, except for that, heaven forgive me, bouncing Amazonian? Your mistress in high boots? Your warrior love is to be married to Theseus. Have you come to bring joy and prosperity to their marital bed?

TITANIA

What, jealous Oberon! Fairies, skip hence; I have forsworn his bed and company.

OBERON

Tarry, rash wanton; am not I thy lord?

TITANIA

Then I must be thy lady; but I know
When thou hast stol'n away from Fairyland,
And in the shape of Corin sat all day
Playing on pipes of corn, and versing love
To amorous Phillida. Why art thou here,
Come from the farthest steepe of India,
But that, forsooth, the bouncing Amazon,
Your buskined mistress and your warrior love,
To Theseus must be wedded, and you come
To give their bed joy and prosperity?

> Note: Corin and Phillida are the names of a shepherd and shepherdess in classical pastoral (religious) poetry.
>
> 'Bouncing Amazon' - suggesting Hippolyta is voluptuous and also suggesting sexual action. 'Buskin' is a thick soled, laced boot worn by Athenian actors to gain height.

OBERON

For shame, Titania! How can you mention my affection for Hippolyta, knowing full well I know about your love for Theseus? Did you not lead him through the glimmering night away from Perigenia, whom he had raped, and encouraged him to cheat on beautiful Aegles with Ariadna and Antiopa?

OBERON

How canst thou thus for shame, Titania,
Glance at my credit with Hippolyta,
Knowing I know thy love to Theseus?
Didst thou not lead him through the glimmering night
From Perigenia, whom he ravished,
And make him with fair Aegles break his faith,
With Ariadne and Antiopa?

> Literary Note: In Greek mythology, Sinis, the father of Perigenia (or Perigouna or Perigune) was killed by Theseus. Perigenia afterwards hid in undergrowth and Theseus was unable to find her. She eventually revealed herself after he promised not to harm her. Theseus then raped her resulting in a male heir, Melanippus. Theseus was married to Phaedra but cheated on his wife with, Aegles, Ariadne (here spelled Ariadna) and Antiopa. Phaedra would hang herself after falling in love with Hippolytus who rejected her. This is taken from Plutarch's "Life of Theseus". Titania did not appear in Plutarch's story, she is a creation of Shakespeare who here makes her responsible for all Theseus' failures in love, as if out of jealousy.

TITANIA

These are figments of your jealousy. And not since the start of midsummer have we met on a hill, or a dale, in forest or meadows, by rocky waterfall or by rushing brook, or on the beaches by the sea, to dance our fairy rings to the whistling of the wind, without you ruining our enjoyment with your arguing. Causing the winds, blowing for us in vain, to seek revenge by sucking up from the sea disease ridden mists which fall on the land, pelting the rivers till they break their banks in flood. The ox have pulled their ploughs in vain, the ploughman sweated for nothing, and the green corn has rotted before it is old enough to mature. Sheep pens stand empty in flooded fields, the crows grow fat on the disease riddled flocks. Games pitches are filled with mud, and the hopscotch outlines on the green are worn away through lack of players. The human mortals want a normal winter here. No night is blessed with the singing of hymns and carols as night and day are now as one. The moon, governess of the tide, pale in her anger, causes rain to fill the air with diseases. And due to this foul weather we have altered seasons. Heavy frosts as the crimson rose blooms, and on winter's thin and icy head the perfumed wreaths of sweet summer buds grow as if in mockery. The spring, the summer, the fruitful autumn, the angry winter, all change their usual apparel, and the bewildered world does not know which is which by the fruits they produce. And these offspring of evil all come from our arguing, from our disagreement. We are the parents of all this.

TITANIA

These are the forgeries of jealousy;
And never, since the middle summer's spring,
Met we on hill, in dale, forest, or mead,
By paved fountain or by rushy brook,
Or in the beached margent of the sea,
To dance our ringlets to the whistling wind,
But with thy brawls thou hast disturbed our sport.
Therefore the winds, piping to us in vain,
As in revenge, have sucked up from the sea
Contagious fogs which, falling in the land,
Hath every pelting river made so proud
That they have overborne their continents.
The ox hath therefore stretched his yoke in vain,
The ploughman lost his sweat, and the green corn
Hath rotted ere his youth attained a beard.
The fold stands empty in the drowned field,
And crows are fatted with the murrion flock;
The nine men's morris is filled up with mud,
And the quaint mazes in the wanton green,
For lack of tread, are undistinguishable.
The human mortals want their winter here;
No night is now with hymn or carol blest;
Therefore the moon, the governess of floods,
Pale in her anger, washes all the air,
That rheumatic diseases do abound.
And thorough this distemperature we see
The seasons alter. Hoary-headed frosts
Fall in the fresh lap of the crimson rose,
And on old Hiems' thin and icy crown
An odorous chaplet of sweet summer buds
Is as in mockery set. The spring, the summer,
The childing autumn, angry winter, change
Their wonted liveries, and the mazed world
By their increase now knows not which is which.
And this same progeny of evils comes
From our debate, from our dissension.
We are their parents and original.

Note: 'Murrion' – murrain, an infectious deadly disease affecting animals.

'Nine men's morris' – A game played by two people on squares marked out in grass. The lines were cut into the grass and they would fill with mud if not tended.

'Quaint mazes' are paths that can be followed on village greens, sometimes of complicated layouts, hence 'maze'. When not used they grow back to normal grass.

'Human mortals' – as opposed to the immortal Titania, Oberon and their fairies.

'Hiem' – Latin for winter.

Trivia: The seasons we know as Spring and Autumn (or Fall) were new to the 16th century, before this only Winter and Summer existed. What we know as Spring was considered early Summer, and Autumn was known as Harvest. No fixed dates existed until recently for the four seasons we now observe. In the 16th century the terms 'the spring of the leaf' and the 'fall of the leaf' were how we came to name the new seasons. The word autumn is derived from Latin 'autumnus'.

OBERON

Why don't you fix it then? The cure lies with you. Why does Titania go against her Oberon? I only beg for a little changeling boy to be my attendant.

TITANIA

Put that thought out of your mind. The whole of fairy land could not buy that child from me. His mother was a follower of mine, and in the spiced Indian evening air has often chatted by my side, and sat with me on Neptune's golden sands watching the trade ships leave on the tide. We have laughed to see the sails billow and grow like pregnant bellies from the seductive wind, which she with her pretty undulating motion – her womb then full of my young child – would imitate, and then she would sail across the land to fetch me treats, and return back again as if from a voyage, laden with goods. But she, being mortal, died in childbirth, and for her sake I am raising her boy, and for her sake I will never part with him.

OBERON

Do you amend it, then; it lies in you.
Why should Titania cross her Oberon?
I do but beg a little changeling boy
To be my henchman.

TITANIA

Set your heart at rest;
The fairy land buys not the child of me.
His mother was a vot'ress of my order;
And in the spiced Indian air by night
Full often hath she gossiped by my side,
And sat with me on Neptune's yellow sands,
Marking th' embarked traders on the flood;
When we have laughed to see the sails conceive
And grow big-bellied with the wanton wind;
Which she, with pretty and with swimming gait
Following -her womb then rich with my young
  squire –
Would imitate, and sail upon the land
To fetch me trifles, and return again,
As from a voyage, rich with merchandise.
But she, being mortal, of that boy did die;
And for her sake do I rear up her boy;
And for her sake I will not part with him.

Note: Neptune was god of the sea in Roman mythology.

OBERON

How long do you intend to stay here in this wood?

TITANIA

Perhaps till after Theseus has married. If you will dance nicely with us in our fairy ring and watch our moonlight revels, you can come with us. If not, shun me, and I will avoid you.

OBERON

Give me that boy and I will go with you.

TITANIA

Not for all fairy land. Fairies, come away!
We'll argue outright if longer I stay.

OBERON

How long within this wood intend you stay?

TITANIA

Perchance till after Theseus' wedding day.
If you will patiently dance in our round
And see our moonlight revels, go with us;
If not, shun me, and I will spare your haunts.

OBERON

Give me that boy and I will go with thee.

TITANIA

Not for thy fairy kingdom. Fairies, away!
We shall chide downright if I longer stay.

EXIT TITANIA WITH HER TRAIN OF FAIRIES.

OBERON

Well, go then, but you shan't leave this grove without suffering for this insult to me.
(*to Puck*) Come here, gentle Puck. You remember the time I sat on a rock and heard a mermaid on a dolphin's back singing with such sweet and harmonious voice that the rough sea grew calm at her song, and certain stars flew madly from their orbits at the sound of the maiden of the sea's music?

OBERON

Well, go thy way; thou shalt not from this grove
Till I torment thee for this injury.
My gentle Puck, come hither. Thou remember'st
Since once I sat upon a promontory,
And heard a mermaid on a dolphin's back
Uttering such dulcet and harmonious breath
That the rude sea grew civil at her song,
And certain stars shot madly from their spheres
To hear the sea-maid's music.

> *Note: Shakespeare again mentions the stars are contained in spheres. See page 38.*

PUCK
I remember.

PUCK
I remember.

OBERON

At the same time, though you could not see him, I saw flying between the cold moon and the earth, cupid, bow in hand. He took careful aim at a beautiful virginal queen of a western isle, and fired his love shaft swiftly from his bow with a force enough to shatter a hundred thousand hearts. But I saw young Cupid's fiery shaft deflected by the watery beams of the virginal moon, and the Imperial Highness passed on in maidenly thought, blissfully unaware. But I marked the spot where Cupid's arrow fell. It fell upon a little English flower, once milky white, now turned purple with love's wound. Maidens call it Idle-love. Fetch me that flower, the bud I showed you once. The juice of it applied to sleeping eyelids will make any man or woman fall madly in love with the first creature they next see. Bring me this flower, and return here before the leviathan can swim a league.

OBERON

That very time I saw, but thou couldst not,
Flying between the cold moon and the earth,
Cupid all armed. A certain aim he took
At a fair vestal throned by the west,
And loosed his love-shaft smartly from his bow
As it should pierce a hundred thousand hearts;
But I might see young Cupid's fiery shaft
Quenched in the chaste beams of the wat'ry moon,
And the imperial vot'ress passed on
In maiden meditation, fancy-free.
Yet marked I where the bolt of Cupid fell.
It fell upon a little western flower,
Before milk-white, now purple with love's wound;
And maidens call it Love-in-idleness.
Fetch me that flower; the herb I showed thee once.
The juice of it on sleeping eyelids laid
Will make or man or woman madly dote
Upon the next live creature that it sees.
Fetch me this herb; and be thou here again
Ere the leviathan can swim a league.

> Note: The virgin queen untouched by cupid's arrow is a famous reference to Queen Elizabeth I. She had private performances of plays performed at her London palaces, as did her successor James I, who was referenced in later plays.
>
> The country 'by the west' is Great Britain. It (if you include Ireland) is the last western isle before the atlantic ocean with no further land mass due west till the 'new world' of the USA. The Mayflower did not set sail for the New World until twenty five years after this play was written.
>
> The white flower turning purple – the colour of blood - is another reference to Thisbe and Pyramus from Ovid's 'Metamorphoses'. The name 'love-in–idleness' is a rural name for a pansy, another name was 'heart's ease'.
>
> Leviathan is a large sea creature, typically a whale, but also mythical sea beasts, and a league is roughly three miles or five kilometres in distance.

PUCK

I'll circle the globe and find it in forty minutes

PUCK

I'll put a girdle round about the earth
In forty minutes.

EXIT PUCK.

OBERON

(*aside*) Once I have this juice I'll watch for when Titania is asleep and drop the juice of it on her eyes. The next thing she sees on waking, be it a lion, bear, wolf, or bull, a meddling monkey or an interfering ape, she will pursue with an obsessive love. And before I remove the spell from her sight, as I can by using a different flower, I'll make her give up her young boy to me. - But who is this coming?

OBERON

Having once this juice,
I'll watch Titania when she is asleep,
And drop the liquor of it in her eyes.
The next thing then she waking looks upon,
Be it on lion, bear, or wolf, or bull,
On meddling monkey, or on busy ape,
She shall pursue it with the soul of love.
And ere I take this charm from off her sight,
As I can take it with another herb,
I'll make her render up her page to me.
But who comes here?

OBERON PLACES A CLOAK FULLY OVER HIMSELF WHICH RENDERS HIM INVISIBLE TO OBSERVERS.

OBERON (CONT'D)

Now I am invisible, and can overhear their conversation.

OBERON

I am invisible,
And I will overhear their conference.

ENTER DEMETRIUS WITH HELENA FOLLOWING BEHIND HIM.

DEMETRIUS

(*to Helena*) I don't love you, so stop following me. Where is Lysander and beautiful Hermia? One of which I'll kill, while the other kills me. You told me they were secretly meeting in this wood. And here I am, in this wood, angry because I cannot meet my Hermia. So go away, follow me no more.

DEMETRIUS

I love thee not, therefore pursue me not.
Where is Lysander and fair Hermia?
The one I'll slay, the other slayeth me.
Thou told'st me they were stol'n unto this wood,
And here am I, and wode within this wood
Because I cannot meet my Hermia.
Hence, get thee gone, and follow me no more.

HELENA

You attract me, you hard-hearted magnet. Though my heart is not hard like iron, my heart is as true as steel. Lose your power of attraction and I will then lose the power to follow you.

HELENA

You draw me, you hard-hearted adamant;
But yet you draw not iron, for my heart
Is true as steel. Leave you your power to draw,
And I shall have no power to follow you.

DEMETRIUS

Do I encourage you? Do I speak to you of love? Or do I instead in the plainest truth tell you that I do not, and I cannot, love you.

DEMETRIUS

Do I entice you? Do I speak you fair?
Or rather do I not in plainest truth
Tell you I do not nor I cannot love you?

HELENA

And even for saying that I love you more. I am your faithful hound, and Demetrius, the more you beat me, the more I will adore you. Use me as your dog, spurn me, strike me, ignore me, abandon me. Just allow me, unworthy though I am, to follow you. What lower level could I beg for your love than to be used as you would use your dog? Yet even that position I would consider to be an honour.

HELENA

And even for that do I love you the more. I am your spaniel; and, Demetrius, The more you beat me I will fawn on you. Use me but as your spaniel, spurn me, strike me, *parallel structure* Neglect me, lose me; only give me leave, Unworthy as I am, to follow you. What worser place can I beg in your love - And yet a place of high respect with me - Than to be used as you use your dog?

> Note: Shakespeare uses the spaniel due to the proverb, 'A spaniel, a woman, a walnut tree / The more you beat them, the truer they be'.

DEMETRIUS

Don't make me hate you any more than I do. It makes me sick to look at you.

DEMETRIUS

Tempt not too much the hatred of my spirit; For I am sick when I do look on thee.

HELENA

And I feel sick when I cannot look at you.

HELENA

And I am sick when I look not on you.

DEMETRIUS

You damage your reputation by leaving the city and throwing yourself into the hands of someone who doesn't love you. To trust the valuable commodity of your virginity to the opportunistic night and the evil intentions so lonely a place attracts.

DEMETRIUS

You do impeach your modesty too much, To leave the city and commit yourself Into the hands of one that loves you not; To trust the opportunity of night And the ill counsel of a desert place With the rich worth of your virginity.

HELENA

Your virtue is my protection, for it is no longer night when I see your face, so I think I am not out at night. Nor does this wood lack worlds of company, for you mean all the world to me. So how can it be said that I am alone when all the world is here to see me?

HELENA

Your virtue is my privilege; for that It is not night when I do see your face, Therefore I think I am not in the night; Nor doth this wood lack worlds of company, For you in my respect are all the world. Then how can it be said I am alone When all the world is here to look on me?

DEMETRIUS

I'll run from you and hide in the bracken, and leave you to the mercy of the wild beasts.

DEMETRIUS

I'll run from thee and hide me in the brakes, And leave thee to the mercy of wild beasts.

HELENA

The wildest beast has not got a heart like yours. Run if you like. The story of Apollo will be reversed, with Apollo fleeing and Daphne doing the chasing. The dove chases the griffin, the timid deer races to catch the tiger – pointless speed when a coward chases and the brave flees.

HELENA

The wildest hath not such a heart as you.
Run when you will; the story shall be changed:
Apollo flies, and Daphne holds the chase;
The dove pursues the griffin; the mild hind
Makes speed to catch the tiger - bootless speed,
When cowardice pursues and valour flies.

DEMETRIUS

I'll not argue with you here. Let me go, because if you follow me, believe me, I'll do you some mischief in the wood.

DEMETRIUS

I will not stay thy questions. Let me go;
Or, if thou follow me, do not believe
But I shall do thee mischief in the wood.

Note: Mischief has the double meaning of doing her physical harm or sexually abusing her - following on from his earlier speech about her virginity in peril.

HELENA

Yes, like you already do me mischief in the church, in the town, in the fields. Really, Demetrius, your offensiveness causes a woman to act scandalously.
We cannot fight for love, as men may do.
We should be wooed, we were not meant to woo.

HELENA

Ay, in the temple, in the town, the field,
You do me mischief. Fie, Demetrius,
Your wrongs do set a scandal on my sex.
We cannot fight for love, as men may do;
We should be wooed, and were not made to woo.

EXIT DEMETRIUS HURRIEDLY.

HELENA (CONT'D)

(aside) I'll follow you, and make heaven of my hell,
To die by the hand which I love so well.

HELENA

I'll follow thee, and make a heaven of hell,
To die upon the hand I love so well.

EXIT HELENA FOLLOWING DEMETRIUS.

OBERON WATCHES THEM LEAVE THEN REMOVES HIS CLOAK TO BECOME VISIBLE AGAIN.

OBERON

Good luck, young maid. Before he leaves this grove
You'll run from him, and he will seek your love.

OBERON

Fare thee well, nymph. Ere he do leave this grove
Thou shalt fly him, and he shall seek thy love.

RE-ENTER PUCK.

OBERON (CONT'D)
Have you got the flower? Welcome back, wanderer.

OBERON
Hast thou the flower there? Welcome, wanderer.

PUCK
Yes, here it is.

PUCK
Ay, there it is.

PUCK PRODUCES A PURPLE PANSY FROM A POUCH.

OBERON
I beg you, give it to me.

OBERON
I pray thee, give it me.

PUCK HANDS OBERON THE FLOWER.

OBERON (CONT'D)
I know a bank where the wild thyme blows,
Where oxslips and the nodding violet grows,
Quite covered over with the lush woodbines,
With sweet scented roses on sharp briar vines.
And there Titania sleeps away the night,
Lulled by the flowers, dancing in delight.
And there the snake casts its bright patterned
  skin,
Full wide enough to wrap a fairy in.

OBERON
I know a bank where the wild thyme blows,
Where oxlips and the nodding violet grows,
Quite over-canopied with luscious woodbine,
With sweet musk-roses, and with eglantine.
There sleeps Titania sometime of the night,
Lulled in these flowers with dances and delight;
And there the snake throws her enamelled skin,
Weed wide enough to wrap a fairy in.

Note: 'Oxlips' are very like cowslips and primroses. Not to be confused (as many do) with the 'false oxlip' which is a cultivated hybrid of the cowslip and the primrose. 'Woodbine' is honeysuckle and 'eglantine' is sweet briar, which is a wild rose.

OBERON HOLDS UP THE FLOWER.

OBERON (CONT'D)
And with the juice of this I'll wet her eyes,
To make her full of horrid fantasies.

OBERON
And with the juice of this I'll streak her eyes,
And make her full of hateful fantasies.

OBERON HANDS PUCK SOME OF THE FLOWER.

Note: The rhyming of 'eyes' and 'fantasies' is explained on page 71.

OBERON (CONT'D)

Here, you take some of it and search this
     grove.
A sweet Arthenian lady is in love
With an indifferent youth. Go wet his eyes.
But do it when the next thing he espies
May be the lady. You will know the man
By the Arthenian clothing he has on.
Now do it with great care so it makes him
More fond of her than she now is of him.
Be sure to meet me ere the first cock's crow.

PUCK

Fear not, my lord, your servant will do so.

OBERON

Take thou some of it, and seek through this grove.
A sweet Athenian lady is in love
With a disdainful youth. Anoint his eyes;
But do it when the next thing he espies
May be the lady. Thou shalt know the man
By the Athenian garments he hath on.
Effect it with some care, that he may prove
More fond on her than she upon her love.
And look thou meet me ere the first cock crow.

PUCK

Fear not, my lord, your servant shall do so.

THEY EXIT IN SEPARATE DIRECTIONS.

ACT II SCENE II

ANOTHER PART OF THE WOOD. NIGHT TIME.

ENTER TITANIA TO HER SLEEPING PLACE WITH HER TRAIN OF FAIRIES.

TITANIA

Come, let's dance a fairy ring and a fairy song, then for the third part of a minute, go - some to kill inchworms in the sweet scented rose buds, some to fight bats for their leather wings to make coats for my small elves, and the others to stop the noisy owl that hoots at night with wonder at our dainty dances.

TITANIA

Come, now a roundel and a fairy song;
Then, for the third part of a minute, hence:
Some to kill cankers in the musk-rose buds,
Some war with reremice for their leathern wings
To make my small elves coats; and some keep back
The clamorous owl that nightly hoots and wonders
At our quaint spirits.

> Note: A 'roundel' is either a dance in a circle, or a song or poem which starts and ends with the same words so it could, if so wished, continue indefinitely.
>
> 'The third part of a minute' is twenty seconds. Shakespeare used the number three and multiples of it when associated with magical creatures as it was considered to have mystical powers, particularly with the witches in Macbeth.
>
> 'Cankers' is short for cankerworms, also known as inchworms, the larvae of the geometer moth. They feed on the buds of plants and are highly destructive.
>
> 'Reremice' is an archaic word for 'bat'.

THEY DANCE AND SING. WHEN FINISHED TITANIA LIES DOWN.

TITANIA

Now sing me to sleep. Then do your tasks and let me rest.

TITANIA

Sing me now asleep;
Then to your offices, and let me rest.

THE FAIRIES SING.

1ST FAIRY

All spotted snakes with double tongues,
  And spiky hedgehogs, don't be seen.
Newts and slow-worms, do no wrongs,
  Come not near our fairy queen.

1ST FAIRY

You spotted snakes with double tongue,
  Thorny hedgehogs, be not seen;
Newts and blind-worms, do no wrong,
  Come not near our fairy queen.

FAIRY CHORUS

Philomel with melody

Join in our sweet lullaby,

  (a nightingale joins in the song)

Lulla-lulla-lullaby, lulla-lulla-lullaby.

Never harm

With spell or charm

Our lovely queen where she lies.

So good night with lullabies.

FAIRY CHORUS

Philomel with melody

Sing in our sweet lullaby;

Lulla, lulla, lullaby, lulla, lulla, lullaby.

Never harm

Nor spell nor charm

Come our lovely lady nigh;

So good night, with lullaby.

Note: Philomel – a nightingale. From Ovid's 'Metamorphoses', where Philomela, the mythical daughter of King Pandion of Athens, was turned into a nightingale to escape her sad plight and gave it its sad song. Many poets and authors were influenced by the story of Philomela including the poet, Keats, and she is referenced in Romeo and Juliet.

1ST FAIRY

Spinning spiders, come not here,

  Go, you daddy long legs, hence!

Beetles black, approach not near,

  Worm nor snail, cause no offence.

1ST FAIRY

Weaving spiders, come not here;

  Hence, you long-legged spinners, hence!

Beetles black, approach not near;

  Worm nor snail, do no offence.

FAIRY CHORUS

Philomel with melody

Join in our sweet lullaby,

Lulla-lulla-lullaby, lulla-lulla-lullaby.

Never harm

With spell or charm

Our lovely queen where she lies.

So good night, with lullabies.

FAIRY CHORUS

Philomel with melody

Sing in our sweet lullaby;

Lulla, lulla, lullaby, lulla, lulla, lullaby.

Never harm

Nor spell nor charm

Come our lovely lady nigh;

So good night, with lullaby.

TITANIA FALLS ASLEEP.

2ND FAIRY

(Hushed)

Now, away! For all is well.

One of you stand sentinel.

2ND FAIRY

Hence, away! Now all is well.

One aloof stand sentinel.

EXIT FAIRIES EXCEPT ONE WHO STANDS GUARD.

ENTER OBERON, INVISIBLE AS HE HAS HIS CLOAK OVER HIM.

HE SQUEEZES THE FLOWER JUICE ON TITANIA'S EYELIDS.

Act II Scene II - Another Part Of The Wood.

OBERON

What you see when you awake,
For your true-love you will take,
You'll love and pine for his sake.
Be it lynx, wild cat, or bear,
Panther, boar with bristly hair,
In your eye what does appear
When you wake, you will love dear.
Awake when some vile thing is near.

OBERON

What thou seest when thou dost wake,
Do it for thy true-love take;
Love and languish for his sake.
Be it ounce, or cat, or bear,
Pard, or boar with bristled hair,
In thy eye that shall appear
When thou wak'st, it is thy dear.
Wake when some vile thing is near.

EXIT OBERON.

ENTER LYSANDER AND HERMIA, MEETING IN SECRET.

LYSANDER

Dear love, you're weak from walking in the
* wood,*
* And, to speak truth, I've forgotten our way.*
We'll rest here, Hermia, if you think it good,
* And hold out for the comfort of the day.*

LYSANDER

Fair love, you faint with wand'ring in the wood;
* And, to speak troth, I have forgot our way.*
We'll rest us, Hermia, if you think it good,
* And tarry for the comfort of the day.*

HERMIA

Good idea Lysander, find yourself a bed,
Here, I, upon this bank will rest my head.

HERMIA

Be it so Lysander. Find you out a bed;
For I upon this bank will rest my head.

LYSANDER

One turf shall be a pillow for us both,
One heart, one bed, two bodies, and one troth.

LYSANDER

One turf shall serve as pillow for us both;
One heart, one bed, two bosoms, and one troth.

Note: A troth is a pledge, typically of marriage.

LYSANDER LIES DOWN NEXT TO HER.

HERMIA

No, good Lysander, for my sake, my dear,
Lie further over there, don't lie so near.

HERMIA

Nay, good Lysander. For my sake, my dear,
Lie further off yet; do not lie so near.

LYSANDER

Oh, trust in me, dear, and my innocence!
True lovers understand without offence.
I meant that my heart unto yours is joined,
So two hearts both as one will be combined.
Two bodies joined together by an oath,
Become as one behind a single troth.
So by your side in bed don't me deny,
As, lying beside you, I do not lie.

LYSANDER

O, take the sense, sweet, of my innocence!
Love takes the meaning in love's conference.
I mean that my heart unto yours is knit,
So that but one heart we can make of it;
Two bosoms interchained with an oath;
So, then, two bosoms and a single troth.
Then by your side no bed-room me deny,
For lying so, Hermia, I do not lie.

HERMIA

Lysander twists words very charmingly.

Much shame upon my manners and my pride
If I, Hermia, had meant Lysander lied.
But, gentle friend, for love and courtesy
Lie further over there for modesty.
A distance such as it can then be said
We are an honest bachelor and a maid,
So move away now, and goodnight, sweet
  friend.
May love be never ending till life's end.

HERMIA

Lysander riddles very prettily.

Now much beshrew my manners and my pride
If Hermia meant to say Lysander lied.
But, gentle friend, for love and courtesy
Lie further off, in human modesty;
Such separation as may well be said
Becomes a virtuous bachelor and a maid,
So far be distant; and good night, sweet friend.
Thy love ne'er alter till thy sweet life end.

LYSANDER MOVES APART FROM HERMIA AND LIES DOWN.

LYSANDER

Amen, amen, to that good prayer, says me,
And end my life if I end loyalty.
Here is my bed. I wish you sleep and rest.

HERMIA

With half that wish, upon you too be blessed.

LYSANDER

Amen, amen to that fair prayer say I;
And then end life when I end loyalty.
Here is my bed. Sleep give thee all his rest.

HERMIA

With half that wish the wisher's eyes be pressed.

Note: A pretty way of saying that she shares the wish with him.

THEY SLEEP.

ENTER PUCK AS IF LOOKING FOR SOMETHING.

PUCK

Through the forest I have gone,
Athenians I found so far – none,
Upon whose eyes I may give
This flower's force in stirring love.
Night and silence... Who's this here?

PUCK

Through the forest have I gone,
But Athenian found I none
On whose eyes I might approve
This flower's force in stirring love.
Night and silence. - Who is here?

PUCK SEES LYSANDER LYING ASLEEP AND GOES TO HIM.

PUCK (CONT'D)

Clothes of Athens he does wear.
He's the one my master said
Disliked the Athenian maid.

PUCK

Weeds of Athens he doth wear.
This is he my master said
Despised the Athenian maid;

PUCK SEES HERMIA LYING A DISTANCE AWAY FROM LYSANDER.

PUCK (CONT'D)

And there's the maiden, sleeping sound,
On the damp and dirty ground.
Pretty thing! - She dares lie not
Near this loveless, heartless clot.
(to the sleeping Lysander)
Low-life, on your eyes I drop
All the power this spell has got.

PUCK

And here the maiden, sleeping sound,
On the dank and dirty ground.
Pretty soul! - she durst not lie
Near this lack-love, this kill-courtesy.
Churl, upon thy eyes I throw
All the power this charm doth owe.

Note: Churl means either a rustic country person with poor manners, or a rude and mean person, mean both with money and in character.

PUCK SQUEEZES THE FLOWER JUICE ON LYSANDER'S EYELIDS.

PUCK (CONT'D)

When you awake, then love forbids
That sleep shall fall on your eyelids.
You'll wake up when I am gone,
I must go now to Oberon.

PUCK

When thou wak'st let love forbid
Sleep his seat on thy eyelid.
So awake when I am gone;
For I must now to Oberon.

EXIT PUCK.

ENTER DEMETRIUS RUNNING, WITH HELENA CHASING BEHIND HIM.

HELENA

(breathless)
Wait, though you'll kill me, dear Demetrius.

HELENA

Stay, though thou kill me, sweet Demetrius.

DEMETRIUS

I order you, stop! Don't haunt me like this.

DEMETRIUS

I charge thee, hence! - and do not haunt me thus.

HELENA

Alone in darkness you would leave me so?

HELENA

O, wilt thou darkling leave me? Do not so.

DEMETRIUS

Stay at your peril, alone I will go.

DEMETRIUS

Stay, on thy peril. I alone will go.

EXIT DEMETRIUS.

HELENA

Oh, I am out of breath in this fool's chase.
The more I beg, the lesser my success.
Hermia is happy, wherever she lies,
For she has been blessed with attractive eyes.
How are her eyes so bright? Not with salt
  tears –
Because mine are washed more often than
  hers.
No, no, I'm as ugly as a great bear,
For creatures that I meet flee me in fear.
So it's no wonder that Demetrius,
As if I'm a monster, flees my presence.
What wicked misleading mirror of spite
Made me think I compared with Hermia's
  sight?

HELENA

O, I am out of breath in this fond chase.
The more my prayer, the lesser is my grace.
Happy is Hermia, wheresoe'er she lies;
For she hath blessed and attractive eyes.
How came her eyes so bright? Not with salt tears -
If so, my eyes are oft'ner washed than hers.
No, no, I am ugly as a bear;
For beasts that meet me run away for fear;
Therefore no marvel though Demetrius
Do as a monster fly my presence thus.
What wicked and dissembling glass of mine
Made me compare with Hermia's sphery eyne?

> Note: 'Eyne' - again Shakespeare uses the poetic word for eyes.

SHE SEES LYSANDER ASLEEP ON THE GROUND.

HELENA

But who is here? Lysander on the ground!
Dead or asleep? I see no blood or wound.
(aloud to Lysander, nudging him)
Lysander if you're alive, good sir, awake.

HELENA

But who is here? Lysander, on the ground?!
Dead, or asleep? I see no blood, no wound.
Lysander, if you live, good sir, awake.

LYSANDER WAKES AND BECOMES TOTALLY SMITTEN WITH HELENA.

LYSANDER

(waking)
And I would run through fire for your dear
  sake.
With fresh eyes I now see you! Nature's art
Which through your bosom makes me see
  your heart.
Where is Demetrius? Oh, how apt a word
Is that vile name to perish by my sword!

LYSANDER

[Waking.]
And run through fire I will for thy sweet sake.
Transparent Helena! Nature shows art
That through thy bosom makes me see thy heart.
Where is Demetrius? O, how fit a word
Is that vile name to perish on my sword!

HELENA

Don't say it, Lysander, do not say that.
Because he loves your Hermia? Lord, so what?
But Hermia still loves you, so content.

HELENA

Do not say so, Lysander; say not so.
What though he love your Hermia? Lord, what though?
Yet Hermia still loves you; then be content.

LYSANDER

Content with Hermia! No, I now resent
The tedious minutes I have with her spent.
Not Hermia but Helena I love.
Who would not swap a raven for a dove?
The mind of man is by reasoning swayed,
And reason says you are the worthier maid.
Young things are not ripe till they reach their
  season,
So I, being young, was unripe to good reason.
Now I've matured to the top of my skill,
Reason has become the guide to my will,
And leads me to your eyes, where I overlook
Love's stories, written in love's sweetest book.

HELENA

Oh, why was I for this mockery born?
When from you did I deserve this scorn?
It's not enough, it's not enough, young man,
That I never did - no, nor never can –
Deserve a sweet look from Demetrius' eye,
That you must then flout my insufficiency?
God's truth, you do me wrong, God's truth you
  do,
In such scornful manner, you come to woo.
So farewell to you. Though I must confess
I thought you a man of more gentleness.
Oh, that a lady by one man refused
Should then by another be so abused!

LYSANDER

Content with Hermia! No; I do repent
The tedious minutes I with her have spent.
Not Hermia but Helena I love:
Who will not change a raven for a dove?
The will of man is by his reason swayed,
And reason says you are the worthier maid.
Things growing are not ripe until their season;
So I, being young, till now ripe not to reason;
And touching now the point of human skill,
Reason becomes the marshal to my will,
And leads me to your eyes, where I o'erlook
Love's stories, written in love's richest book.

HELENA

Wherefore was I to this keen mockery born?
When at your hands did I deserve this scorn?
Is't not enough, is't not enough, young man,
That I did never - no, nor never can -
Deserve a sweet look from Demetrius' eye,
But you must flout my insufficiency?
Good troth, you do me wrong, good sooth, you do,
In such disdainful manner me to woo.
But fare you well. Perforce I must confess
I thought you lord of more true gentleness.
O, that a lady of one man refused
Should of another therefore be abused!

LYSANDER

She saw not Hermia. - Hermia, stay asleep,
And never Lysander's company keep!
Overindulgence of the sweetest things
The sickest feeling to the stomach it brings,
Or as the vices that men do succumb
Are hated most by those they overwhelm,
So you, my surfeit and my depravity,
May be hated by all, but mostly by me!
And, all my powers, use your strength and
  might,
To honour Helena, and be her knight!

LYSANDER

She see not Hermia. Hermia, sleep thou there,
And never mayst thou come Lysander near!
For as a surfeit of the sweetest things
The deepest loathing to the stomach brings,
Or as the heresies that men do leave
Are hated most of those they did deceive,
So thou, my surfeit and my heresy,
Of all be hated, but the most of me!
And, all my powers, address your love and might
To honour Helen, and to be her knight!

EXIT LYSANDER FOLLOWING HELENA.

HERMIA AWAKES.

HERMIA

Help me, Lysander, help me! Do your best
To pluck this crawling serpent from my
    breast!
Oh piteous me, the dream I had here!
Lysander, look how I'm shaking in fear.
A serpent I thought had eaten my heart,
And sat there smiling at his cruel art.
Lysander! What, gone? Lysander! My lord!
What, cannot hear me? Gone? No sound, no
    word?
Alas, where are you? Speak if you can hear.
Speak, in the name of love! I faint with fear.
No? Then I assume you are not close by.
I must quickly find you or here I will die.

HERMIA

[Waking.] Help me, Lysander, help me! Do thy best
To pluck this crawling serpent from my breast!
Ay me, for pity! What a dream was here!
Lysander, look how I do quake with fear.
Methought a serpent ate my heart away,
And you sat smiling at his cruel prey.
Lysander! What, removed? Lysander! Lord!
What, out of hearing? Gone? No sound, no word?
Alack, where are you? Speak, an if you hear.
Speak, of all loves! I swoon almost with fear.
No? Then I well perceive you are not nigh.
Either death or you I'll find immediately.

EXIT HERMIA TO SEARCH FOR LYSANDER, LEAVING ONLY TITANIA ASLEEP AND
HER FAIRY STANDING GUARD OVER HER.

ACT III

A WOOD NEAR ATHENS

LORD, WHAT FOOLS THESE MORTALS BE!

ACT III

ACT III SCENE I

A WOOD NEAR ATHENS. THE SAME NIGHT.

TITANIA IS STILL LYING ASLEEP.

ENTER THE CLOWNS: QUINCE, SNUG, BOTTOM, FLUTE, SNOUT, AND STARVELING.

Note: The comedians (Clowns), get their words mixed up at times for comedic purposes, known as a 'blunder', and signified by italics.

The clowns speak in prose to signify this is a light hearted break. Most of the original language is retained in the translation as it is understandable and was intentionally badly worded.

BOTTOM Are we all here?	BOTTOM Are we all met?
QUINCE Right on time. And here's a *marvellous* convenient place for our rehearsal. This open green will be our stage, this hawthorn bush our dressing room, and we'll do the actions as we'll do them before the Duke.	QUINCE Pat, pat; and here's a marvellous convenient place for our rehearsal. This green plot shall be our stage, this hawthorn-brake our tiring-house; and we will do it in action as we will do it before the duke.

Note: 'Pat, pat' – In the nick of time/at exactly the right moment. Pat also means 'off by heart', as in the expression, 'have something down pat'. This could be word play on the fact they should have learnt their lines before meeting. i.e. on time and memorized.

BOTTOM Peter Quince!	BOTTOM Peter Quince!
QUINCE What is it, Bully Bottom?	QUINCE What sayst thou, Bully Bottom?

Note: 'Bully' was used as a familiar term of friendship. It did not take on the current meaning of intimidation until the 19th century.

BOTTOM

There are things in this here *comedy* tragedy of Pyramus and Thisbe that won't please them. First, Pyramus must draw a sword and kill himself, which will upset the ladies. What answer do you have to that?

BOTTOM

There are things in this comedy of Pyramus and Thisbe that will never please. First, Pyramus must draw a sword to kill himself; which the ladies cannot abide. How answer you that? *problem 1*

> Note: The story of Pyramus and Thisbe is quite obviously a tragedy, not a comedy, the storyline not being too dissimilar to that of Romeo and Juliet.

SNOUT

By heavens, a *perlous* perilous worry.

SNOUT

By'r-lakin, a parlous fear.

> Note: "By'r-lakin" – a mild exclamation of shock. A corruption of "by our little lady", the lady being the Virgin Mary, mother of Jesus Christ.
>
> He mispronounces 'perilous', used by Shakespeare in other plays for comic effect.

STARVELING

I think we must leave the killing out, when all is said and done.

STARVELING

I believe we must leave the killing out, when all is done.

BOTTOM

Not a bit. I have an idea to make it work. Write me a prologue, and let the prologue seem to say that we will do no harm with our swords, and that Pyramus is not killed indeed, and, for the more better assurance, tell them that I, Pyramus, am not Pyramus, but Bottom the weaver. This will take the fear out of them.

BOTTOM

Not a whit. I have a device to make all well. Write me a prologue; and let the prologue seem to say we will do no harm with our swords, and that Pyramus is not killed indeed; and, for the more better assurance, tell them that I, Pyramus, am not Pyramus, but Bottom the weaver. This will put them out of fear.

> Note: "Whit" – a very small amount.

QUINCE

Well, we can have such a prologue, and it shall be written in alternate eight and six beats per line.

QUINCE

Well, we will have such a prologue; and it shall be written in eight and six.

BOTTOM

No, make it two more. Let all lines be eight beats.

BOTTOM

No, make it two more. Let it be written in eight and eight.

SNOUT

Will the ladies not be afraid of the lion?

SNOUT

Will not the ladies be afeard of the lion? *problem 2*

STARVELING

It scares me, I promise you.

BOTTOM

Gentlemen, you should consider with yourselves, that to bring in – God help us! – a lion among ladies is a most dreadful thing, for there is no more frightening wild *fowl* alive than your lion, and we ought to think about it.

STARVELING

I fear it, I promise you.

BOTTOM

Masters, you ought to consider with yourself: to bring in - God shield us! - a lion among ladies is a most dreadful thing; for there is not a more fearful wild-fowl than your lion living; and we ought to look to't.

> Note: He probably means wild beast, not wild fowl (bird). A Shakespeare joke.
>
> This is based on an actual event at the Scottish Court in 1594, at the christening of Prince Henry. A celebratory chariot was pulled in by a blackamoor (a dark skinned African) because it was feared that the lion which had originally been intended to pull it, might frighten the lady spectators, especially if the lighted torches 'drove the lion to fury'.

SNOUT

Therefore another prologue must explain he is not a lion.

BOTTOM

No, you must say his name, and half his face must be seen through the lion's head, and he must speak through it saying this, or to some same *defect* affect . "Ladies", or "Fair ladies, I would wish you", or "I would request you", or "I would beg you not to fear, nor to tremble. I stake my life on yours being safe! If you think I come here as a lion, it would be the regret of my life. No, I am no such thing. I am a man just as other men are". And there, indeed, let him name his name, and tell them plainly he is Snug the carpenter.

SNOUT

Therefore another prologue must tell he is not a lion.

BOTTOM

Nay, you must name his name, and half his face must be seen through the lion's neck, and he himself must speak through saying thus, or to the same defect: `Ladies', or `Fair ladies, I would wish you', or `I would request you', or `I would entreat you not to fear, not to tremble. My life for yours! If you think I come hither as a lion, it were pity of my life. No, I am no such thing; I am a man as other men are'. And there, indeed, let him name his name, and tell them plainly he is Snug the joiner.

> Note: Again, this is based on an actual event, recorded in a notebook of anecdotes and jests by Nicholas Le Strange. The excerpt reads, "There was a spectacle presented to Queen Elizabeth upon the water, and among others Harry Goldingham was to represent Arion upon the dolphin's backe; but finding his voice to be verye hoarse and unpleasant, when he came to perform it, he tears off his disguise, and swears he was none of Arion, not lie, but even honest Harry Goldingham; which blunt discoverie pleased the queene better than if he had gone through in the right way".

QUINCE

Well, it shall be so. But there *is* two difficult things: that is - to bring the moonlight into a room, for you know, Pyramus and Thisbe meet by moonlight.

QUINCE

Well, it shall be so. But there is two hard things: that is, to bring the moonlight into a chamber; for, you know, Pyramus and Thisbe meet by moonlight.

problem 3

SNOUT

Does the moon shine the night we play our play?

SNOUT

Doth the moon shine that night we play our play?

BOTTOM

A calendar, a calendar! Look in the almanac. Look up moonshine, look up moonshine.

BOTTOM

A calendar, a calendar! Look in the almanac. Find out moonshine, find out moonshine.

Note: An almanac is an annual calendar containing important dates and statistical information such as astronomical data and tide tables. The reason Quince conveniently had one to hand is that back then there were no portable time pieces, people based their timing around the sun and the moon. The moon's phase and the sun's equinox were particularly important to them. The opening night of the Globe Theatre and the play Julius Caesar were both determined by the moon's phase. Due to the recent changing of the calendar from Julian to Gregorian, it could no longer be annual dates that were followed, and there were many strong superstitions about doing things during a certain moon's phase. Only move house on a new moon was one, as King Lear observes when he plans his moves between his daughter's houses. It was common to carry an Almanac which tabled sun rise and sunset or an Ephemeredes which charted with high accuracy the positions of the stars and the planets, and the phase of the moon. These both came in the form of a single page pamphlet and were carried upon the person, and both overlapped information depending on the printer.

QUINCE PRODUCES A SINGLE SHEET ALMANAC AND STUDIES IT.

QUINCE

Yes, it does shine that night.

QUINCE

Yes, it doth shine that night.

BOTTOM

In that case, you may leave a skylight of the great chamber window where we play, open, and the moon may shine in at the skylight.

BOTTOM

Why, then may you leave a casement of the great chamber window, where we play, open, and the moon may shine in at the casement.

QUINCE

Yes, or else someone must come in with a bush of thorns and a lantern and say he comes to *disfigure*, badly impersonate or to *present*, represent the personage of Moonshine.

QUINCE

Ay; or else one must come in with a bush of thorns and a lantern and say he comes to disfigure, or to present, the person of Moonshine.

Note: Some editors claim that 'disfigure' is a blunder for 'prefigure', which meant 'imagine beforehand'. It makes less sense than taking it in its literal sense of 'spoiling the appearance' of the moon, being that it's man in a bush. The man in the moon was believed in folklore to be the man caught gathering sticks on the Sabbath and sentenced by God to death by stoning in the Bible, Numbers XV 32–36.

QUINCE (CONT'D)

Then there is another thing, we must have a wall in the great chamber, because Pyramus and Thisbe - says the story - talked through the chink in a wall.

QUINCE

Then there is another thing: we must have a wall in the great chamber; for Pyramus and Thisbe, says the story, did talk through the chink of a wall.

problem

Note: Pyramus and Thisbe lived in adjoining houses. Forbidden to see each other, they made a hole (a chink) in the wall separating them in order to communicate.

SNOUT

You could never bring a wall. What say you, Bottom?

SNOUT

You can never bring in a wall. What say you, Bottom?

BOTTOM

Some man or other must *present* represent Wall. And let him have some plaster or some clay, or some cement coating on him to signify a Wall. And let him hold his fingers like so...

BOTTOM

Some man or other must present Wall; and let him have some plaster, or some loam, or some rough-cast about him, to signify Wall; and let him hold his fingers thus,

He demonstrates with his fingers an opening in the wall through which the actors may talk.

BOTTOM (CONT'D)

And through that opening Pyramus and Thisbe can whisper.

BOTTOM

and through that cranny shall Pyramus and Thisbe whisper.

QUINCE

It that case, then all is well. Come, sit down, every mother's son of you, and rehearse your parts. Pyramus, you begin. When you have spoken your speech, go into the thicket, and likewise everyone according to his cue.

QUINCE

If that may be, then all is well. Come, sit down, every mother's son, and rehearse your parts. Pyramus, you begin. When you have spoken your speech, enter into that brake; and so everyone according to his cue.

ENTER PUCK BEHIND THEM.

PUCK

(aside) What unkemp rustics have we showing off here, so near to the bed of the Fairy Queen? - What? Preparing for a play! I'll be a critic. An actor too, if I can find a way.

PUCK

[Aside.] What hempen homespuns have we swagg'ring here,
So near the cradle of the Fairy Queen?
What, a play toward! I'll be an auditor;
An actor too, perhaps, if I see cause.

QUINCE

Speak, Pyramus. Thisbe, take your place.

QUINCE

Speak, Pyramus. Thisbe, stand forth.

PYRAMUS (BOTTOM) AND THISBE (FLUTE) TAKE THEIR PLACES.

THE OTHERS STAY SEATED TO WAIT THEIR CUE.

BOTTOM STARTS ACTING THE ROLE OF PYRAMUS.

BOTTOM

(as Pyramus) "Thisbe, the flowers of odious scents so sweet"...

BOTTOM

"Thisbe, the flowers of odious savours sweet" -

QUINCE

(interrupting and correcting him)
Odorous! Odorous!

QUINCE

Odours, odours.

BOTTOM

"... odorous scents so sweet,
So like your breath, my dearest Thisbe dear.
But hark, a voice. You stay here for awhile,
And very soon I will again appear.

BOTTOM

"- odours savours sweet;
So hath thy breath, my dearest Thisbe dear.
But hark, a voice. Stay thou but here awhile,
And by and by I will to thee appear."

EXIT BOTTOM BEHIND THE IMPROMPTU THICKET DRESSING ROOM.

PUCK

This is the strangest Pyramus ever performed.

PUCK

A stranger Pyramus than e'er played here.

EXIT PUCK. FLUTE (AS THISBE) STANDS SILENT. QUINCE GLARES AT HIM.

FLUTE

Must I speak now?

FLUTE

Must I speak now?

QUINCE

Aye, indeed you must. For you must understand he goes to *see* the noise that he heard, and is to come back again.

QUINCE

Ay, marry must you; for you must understand he goes but to see a noise that he heard, and is to come again.

Note: You can't of course see a noise, this is intentional miswording for comedy.

FLUTE

(as Thisbe) "Most radiant Pyramus, most lily-
    white of hue,
    Of colour like the red rose on the rearing
    briar,
Most energetic youth, and also most lovely
    Jew,
    As true as the truest horse that would never
    tire,
I'll meet you, Pyramus, at Ninny's tomb."

FLUTE

"Most radiant Pyramus, most lily-white of hue,
    Of colour like the red rose on triumphant brier,
Most brisky juvenal, and eke most lovely Jew,
    As true as truest horse that yet would never tire,
I'll meet thee, Pyramus, at Ninny's tomb."

> Note: 'Triumphant brier' – a thorny rose briar rearing itself aloft.
>
> 'Brisky' - briskly, energetic. 'Juvenal' - juvenile or young. (Juvenal was a Roman satirist but it was not him being referred to here).
>
> 'Eke' is an archaic term for 'also'. (It now means to act frugally or manage with little)
>
> 'Jew' – used to alliterate with 'juvenal' and to rhyme with hew. Flute was probably meant to say 'jewel' but he got the word wrong. If we take into consideration that at the time of writing Jews were unliked in England (and not very common) and it was used as a derogatory term that would not be associated with the word 'lovely'. The audience of the day would have recognised this as a joke.

QUINCE

(admonishing Flute) Ninus' tomb, man!
But you must not speak that part yet! That
is your answer to Pyramus. You've spoken
all your parts at once, cues as well.
(calling to Pyramus) Pyramus! – enter,
you've missed your cue. It is "never tire".

QUINCE

Ninus' tomb, man! Why, you must not speak that
    yet. That you answer to Pyramus. You speak all
    your part at once, cues and all. Pyramus! - enter,
    your cue is past. It is `never tire.'

> Note: When Thisbe says the words "never tire" Pyramus is meant to reappear on stage, but Bottom missed his cue.

FLUTE REPEATS THE LINE TO CUE IN BOTTOM, EMPHASISING THE CUE WORDS,
"NEVER TIRE".

FLUTE

Oh!

"As true as the truest horse that would **never
    tire**".

FLUTE

O!

"As true as truest horse, that yet would never tire".

RE-ENTER PUCK, HE MAGICALLY PUTS AN ASS HEAD ON BOTTOM.

RE-ENTER BOTTOM, NOW WITH AN ASS'S HEAD, BUT HE DOESN'T KNOW IT.

66

BOTTOM

"If I were beautiful, Thisbe, I were only yours."

BOTTOM

"If I were fair, Thisbe, I were only thine."

> Note: Bottom has obviously read the line incorrectly. It should say, "If I were, beautiful Thisbe, I were only yours" – calling Thisbe beautiful. Instead he calls himself beautiful. Some productions make this more obvious by having him say the first part incorrectly, and then having him repeat it as it should have been spoken. But all this is generally lost because of the bizarre head he now has.

THE GROUP OF ACTORS (CLOWNS) REACT IN HORROR AT BOTTOM APPEARING
WITH WHAT APPEARS TO BE A REAL ASS'S HEAD AND TALKING.

QUINCE

Oh, monstrous! Oh, madness! We are haunted! Quick, Men! Flee, Men! Help!

QUINCE

O monstrous! O strange! We are haunted! Pray, masters! Fly, masters! Help!

EXEUNT QUINCE, SNUG, FLUTE, SNOUT AND STARVELING AT PACE.

BOTTOM IS LEFT STANDING AMAZED.

PUCK

(aside, about the fleeing men)
I'll follow you, I'll lead you round and around,
* Through bog, through bush, through gorse,*
*   through briar,*
Sometimes I'm a horse, sometimes a hound,
* Or a hog, a headless bear, sometimes a fire.*
I'll neigh, I'll bark, I'll grunt and roar and
*   burn,*
Like horse, hound, hog, bear, or fire at every
*   turn.*

PUCK

I'll follow you, I'll lead you about a round,
Through bog, through bush, through brake, through briar;
Sometime a horse I'll be, sometime a hound,
A hog, a headless bear, sometime a fire;
And neigh, and bark, and grunt, and roar, and burn,
Like horse, hound, hog, bear, fire, at every turn.

> Note: 'A fire' – he means a 'will-o'-the-wisp'. In folklore a will-o'-the wisp, or a jack-o'-lantern, was a name given to an atmospheric light which appears in the air with no obvious explanation, particularly over bogs, swamps and marshes. It is a common natural phenomenon, but unexplained in Shakespeare's time. Folklore said it was to mislead travellers by resembling a flickering lantern.

EXIT PUCK AFTER THE FRIGHTENED MEN.

BOTTOM

Why did they run away? This is trickery of theirs to scare me.

BOTTOM

Why do they run away? This is a knavery of them to make me afeard.

RE-ENTER SNOUT, CAUTIOUSLY.

SNOUT

Oh, Bottom, you have changed! What's that I see on you?

BOTTOM

What do you see? You see an ass-head like your own, do you?

SNOUT

O Bottom, thou art changed! What do I see on thee?

BOTTOM

What do you see? You see an ass-head of your own, do you?

EXIT SNOUT, RUNNING AWAY.

RE-ENTER QUINCE AT A DISTANCE TAKING ANOTHER LOOK.

QUINCE

May God bless you, Bottom, bless you! You are transformed.

QUINCE

Bless thee, Bottom, bless thee! Thou art translated.

EXIT QUINCE, QUICKLY.

BOTTOM

I can see through their trickery. This is to make an ass of me, to frighten me. But I will not move from this place, let them do what they will. I will walk up and down here, and I will sing so they will hear I am not afraid.

(*sings*)

The blackbird that's so dark of hue,
* With orange coloured bill,*
The song thrush with its note so true,
* The wren with tiny trill.*

BOTTOM

I see their knavery. This is to make an ass of me, to fright me, if they could. But I will not stir from this place, do what they can. I will walk up and down here, and I will sing, that they shall hear I am not afraid.

[Sings.]   *The ousel cock so black of hue,*
* With orange-tawny bill,*
The throstle with his note so true,
* The wren with little quill;*

TITANIA AWAKES AT THE SINGING.

TITANIA

What angel wakes me in my flowery bed?

BOTTOM

(*sings*) *The finch, the sparrow, and the lark,*
* The tuneless cuckoo grey,*
Whose song which many a man does mark,
* But dares not answer "Nay!"...*

TITANIA

What angel wakes me from my flowery bed?

BOTTOM

[Sings.]   *The finch, the sparrow, and the lark,*
* The plain-song cuckoo grey,*
Whose note full many a man doth mark,
* And dares not answer Nay –*

Note: The sound of the cuckoo was used to signify a man who was a cuckold. It was used to torment a man whose wife had been unfaithful. Many men feared the sound because they could not argue 'Nay, I am not a cuckold'. 'Nay' means no and is also the sound a donkey would make.

BOTTOM (CONT'D

For indeed, who would match his wits with so foolish a bird? Who would tell the bird it is lying, however often it cried 'cuckoo' endlessly.

TITANIA

I beg you, gentle mortal, sing again. My ear is much enamoured by your voice, and my eye is enthralled by your beauty.
And modesty's force cannot prevent me
On first sight, swearing my love to thee.

BOTTOM

I think, madam, you should have little reason for that. And yet, to tell the truth, reason and love have little in common nowadays, the more's the pity that some honest acquaintances do not make them friends. No, I joke about it on occasions.

TITANIA

You are as wise as you are beautiful.

BOTTOM

Not so, I'm neither. But if I had brains enough to get out of this wood, I'd be happy with what I had.

TITANIA

Out of this wood, you will not wish to go.
You'll remain here, whether you say yes or no.
I am a spirit of much high appraise
The summer follows me, with me it stays.
And I do love you, so follow me please,
To serve you I'll give you your own fairies.
And they shall fetch you jewels from the deep,
And sing to you while on pressed flowers you
* sleep.*
And I'll remove your mortal limits so
That airy like a spirit you will go.

BOTTOM

For indeed, who would set his wit to so foolish a bird? Who would give a bird the lie, though he cry ' cuckoo' never so?

TITANIA

I pray thee, gentle mortal, sing again;
Mine ear is much enamoured of thy note.
So is mine eye enthralled to thy shape;
And thy fair virtue's force perforce doth move me
On the first view to say, to swear, I love thee.

BOTTOM

Methinks, mistress, you should have little reason *the most the play* for that. And yet, to say the truth, reason and love keep little company together nowadays; the more the pity that some honest neighbours will not make them friends. Nay, I can gleek upon occasion.

TITANIA

Thou art as wise as thou art beautiful.

BOTTOM

Not so, neither; but if I had wit enough to get out of this wood, I have enough to serve mine own turn.

TITANIA

Out of this wood do not desire to go;
Thou shalt remain here, whither thou wilt or no.
I am a spirit of no common rate;
The summer still doth tend upon my state;
And I do love thee; therefore, go with me.
I'll give thee fairies to attend on thee;
And they shall fetch thee jewels from the deep,
And sing while thou on pressed flowers dost sleep;
And I will purge thy mortal grossness so
That thou shalt like an airy spirit go.

Note: 'From the deep' – from the depths of the ocean.

'Moth' was pronounced 'mote'. As is still the custom in parts of the UK and particularly southern Ireland when pronouncing the soft 'th' as a hard 't'.

TITANIA STANDS AND CLAPS HER HANDS, CALLING TO HER FAIRIES.

TITANIA
(*calls*) Peaseblossom! Cobweb! Moth! And Mustardseed!

TITANIA
Peaseblossom! Cobweb! Moth! and Mustardseed!

ENTER FOUR FAIRIES; PEASEBLOSSOM, COBWEB, MOTH, AND MUSTARDSEED.

PEASEBLOSSOM
Ready.

PEASEBLOSSOM
Ready.

COBWEB
And me.

COBWEB
And I.

MOTH
And me.

MOTH
And I.

MUSTARDSEED
And me.

MUSTARDSEED
And I.

ALL
What shall we do?

ALL
Where shall we go?

TITANIA
Be kind and courteous to this gentleman.
Hop, skip and jump, before his very eyes,
Feed him with apricots and dewberries,
And purple grapes, green figs, and mulberries.
Steal honey sacs from humming bumble bees,
For night lights do remove their waxen thighs,
And light them from the burning glow-worm's
  fires,
To lead my love to bed, till he does rise.
And pluck the wings from painted butterflies,
To keep the moonbeams from his sleeping
  eyes.
And bow and scrape, elves, do him courtesies.

TITANIA
Be kind and courteous to this gentleman;
Hop in his walks and gambol in his eyes;
Feed him with apricocks and dewberries,
With purple grapes, green figs, and mulberries.
The honey-bags steal from the humble-bees,
And for night-tapers crop their waxen thighs,
And light them at the fiery glow-worm's eyes,
To have my love to bed and to arise;
And pluck the wings from painted butterflies,
To fan the moonbeams from his sleeping eyes.
Nod to him, elves, and do him courtesies.

Note: 'Honey-bags' – what we know as pollen sacs in which bees collect pollen to take back to the hive and make honey. There is no honey carried in the sacs, this is either poetic whimsy or the mechanics of bees was misunderstood by Shakespeare.

Cutting off the wax covered legs of bees to use as wicks (tapers) for light. While beeswax is very good for making candles it is another flight of fancy to believe the bees have accumulated enough wax on their legs to make a useful wick.

'Glow-worm's eyes' – here the word 'eye' is used to poetically signify the point at which the glow concentrates. Not the eye of the glow worm itself. Rather like saying 'the eye of the storm'.

Again, Shakespeare rhymes 'eye' with a word we would pronounce ending in an 'ee' sound. In Shakespeare's day, this would have been a perfect rhyme. The technical reason for this is 'secondary stress'. Take Helena's line earlier for example, "My ear should catch your voice, my eye your eye, / My tongue should catch your tongue's sweet melody. Eye is rhymed with melody. This was commonplace in Middle English, especially in poetry. The word 'melody' would have a secondary stress on the final syllable '-dy', pronouncing it 'die', which of course rhymes with 'eye'. However, in the speech above, Shakespeare also rhymes 'mulberries' with 'bees', meaning the actor either had to pronounce 'bee' as 'bye' to conform with the other lines, or ignore the rule completely and make both end in an 'ee' sound.

PEASEBLOSSOM	PEASEBLOSSOM
Greetings, mortal!	Hail, mortal!
COBWEB	COBWEB
Greetings!	Hail!
MOTH	MOTH
Greetings!	Hail!
MUSTARDSEED	MUSTARDSEED
Greetings!	Hail!

BOTTOM TRIES TO SOUND EDUCATED AS HE SPEAKS TO THE FAIRIES.

BOTTOM	BOTTOM
(*to Cobweb, trying to sound educated*)	I cry your worships mercy, heartily. I beseech your
I beg your honourable pardon, but may I enquire as to your name?	worship's name.
COBWEB	COBWEB
Cobweb.	Cobweb.
BOTTOM	BOTTOM
I shall desire you to be of better acquaintance, good Mr Cobweb. If I cut my finger I shall make good use of your web.	I shall desire you of more acquaintance, good Master Cobweb. If I cut my finger I shall make bold with you.

Note: Cobwebs were used to bind cuts, like a primitive sticking plaster.

BOTTOM (CONT'D)
(*to Peaseblossom*) And your name, honest gentleman?

PEASEBLOSSOM
Peaseblossom.

BOTTOM
I pray you commend me to your mother, Mrs Squash, and to Mr Peaspod, your father. Good Mr Peaseblossom, I shall desire you to be of more acquaintance too.

BOTTOM
Your name, honest gentleman?

PEASEBLOSSOM
Peaseblossom.

BOTTOM
I pray you, commend me to Mistress Squash, your mother, and to Master Peascod, your father. Good Master Peaseblossom, I shall desire you of more acquaintance too.

> *Note: A 'Peascod' is a ripe pod of peas. A 'squash' is a soft fleshy vegetable, but back then it was also an unripe pod of peas, what we now know as 'mange-tout'. 'Peaseblossom' is the flower of the pea plant.*

BOTTOM (CONT'D)
(*to Mustardseed*) Your name, I beseech you, sir?

MUSTARDSEED
Mustardseed.

BOTTOM
Good Mr Mustardseed, I know well what you have to endure. The cowardly giant beef steak has devoured many gentlemen from your family. I promise you, your relatives have made my eyes water before now. I desire more of your acquaintance, good Mr Mustardseed.

TITANIA
Come, tend to him, lead him to my room,
 The moon, I think, looks on with wat'ry eye.
And when she weeps, so too does every bloom,
 In sadness at my enforced chastity.

BOTTOM
Your name, I beseech you, sir?

MUSTARDSEED
Mustardseed.

BOTTOM
Good Master Mustardseed, I know your patience well. That same cowardly, giant-like ox-beef hath devoured many a gentleman of your house. I promise you your kindred hath made my eyes water ere now. I desire your more acquaintance, good Master Mustardseed.

TITANIA
Come, wait upon him; lead him to my bower.
The moon, methinks, looks with a watery eye;
And when she weeps, weeps every little flower,
Lamenting some enforced chastity.

BOTTOM MAKES THE NOISE OF AN ASS BRAYING.

TITANIA (CONT'D)
Tie up my love's tongue, bring him silently.

TITANIA
Tie up my love's tongue; bring him silently.

ACT III SCENE II

ANOTHER PART OF THE WOOD. THE SAME NIGHT.

Note: This scene is long and rather farce-like, with characters coming and going, and sleeping and waking at a rapid pace.

ENTER KING OF THE FAIRIES, (OBERON) WITH PUCK NOT FAR BEHIND.

OBERON	OBERON
I wonder if Titania has awakened,	I wonder if Titania be awaked;
And what it was that first came to her eye.	*Then what it was that next came in her eye,*
Which she must love in most extremity	*Which she must dote on in extremity.*
Here comes my messenger.	Here comes my messenger.
(to Puck) How are you, mad spirit!	How now, mad spirit!
What night time news have you about this grove?	*What night-rule now about this haunted grove?*

Note: 'Haunted' in this sense is a frequented place, as in, one of his favourite haunts.

PUCK	PUCK
My mistress with a monster is in love.	*My mistress with a monster is in love.*
By her secret and most sacred bower,	*Near to her close and consecrated bower,*
While she was in her lull and sleeping hour,	*While she was in her dull and sleeping hour,*
A bunch of fools, crude men in overalls,	*A crew of patches, rude mechanicals*
That earn their bread back in Athenian halls,	*That work for bread upon Athenian stalls,*
Had met together to rehearse a play,	*Were met together to rehearse a play*
Intended for great Theseus' wedding day.	*Intended for great Theseus' nuptial day.*

Note: 'Consecrated' – dedicated to the purpose.

'Bower' – has the double meaning of an enclosed sheltered place outdoors, and a woman's bed chamber. It derives from the German 'bauer', meaning 'birdcage'.

'Patches' – fools, clowns. The name comes from the coloured, patched outfits which jesters wore.

'Mechanicals' – working tradesmen.

'Athenian stalls' – where they ply their trade in Athens, workshops etc.

PUCK (CONT'D)

The stupidest blockhead of that motley lot
Who played Pyramus, in their on-stage plot
Left the stage and hid behind some bracken,
Where he found I'd his advantage taken,
An ass's bonce I fixed about his head.
Soon, at his cue when Thisbe's lines were read,
Then out this actor comes, and all men see,
Like wild geese from a poacher they all flee,
Like dark grey headed jackdaws in a gang,
Will rise up screeching at a gun's loud bang,
Disperse themselves and madly sweep the sky,
So, likewise, seeing him, his friends did fly.
And as they run, then o'er and o'er one falls,
He cries out loud, then help from Athens calls.
Their senses weak, lost in their fears so strong,
And thinking lifeless things can do them
wrong.
The briars and the thorns their clothing
scratch,
Some sleeves, some hats from wearers they do
snatch.
I led them on in this distracted fear,
And left Pyramus newly transformed there.
When at that moment, so it came to pass,
Titania wakes up, smitten by an ass.

PUCK

The shallowest thickskin of that barren sort,
Who Pyramus presented, in their sport
Forsook his scene and entered in a brake.
When I did him at this advantage take,
An ass's nole I fixed on his head.
Anon his Thisbe must be answered,
And forth my mimic comes. When him they spy -
As wild geese that the creeping fowler eye,
Or russet-pated choughs, many in sort,
Rising and cawing at the gun's report,
Sever themselves and madly sweep the sky -
So, at his sight, away his fellows fly,
And, at our stamp, here o'er and o'er one falls;
He murder cries, and help from Athens calls.
Their sense thus weak, lost with their fears thus strong,
Made senseless things begin to do them wrong;
For briars and thorns at their apparel snatch;
Some sleeves, some hats, from yielders all things catch.
I led them on in this distracted fear,
And left sweet Pyramus translated there;
When in that moment, so it came to pass,
Titania waked, and straightway loved an ass.

OBERON

This works out better than I could devise.
But have you yet smeared the Athenian's eyes
With the love juice, as I ordered you?

OBERON

This falls out better than I could devise.
But hast thou yet latched the Athenian's eyes
With a love-juice, as I did bid thee do?

Note: 'Latched' – the word here was probably meant to be 'hatched' in its rarer older meaning of 'stained' or 'smeared'. 'Hatched' is also used in this sense in Twelfth Night.

PUCK

I found him sleeping – that is done now too –
With the Athenian woman by his side,
So, when he wakes, then she must be espied.

PUCK

I took him sleeping - that is finished too -
And the Athenian woman by his side,
That, when he waked, of force she must be eyed.

ENTER HERMIA AND DEMETRIUS.

OBERON

Stand back. This is the same Athenian.

OBERON

Stand close. This is the same Athenian.

Act III Scene II - Another Part Of The Wood.

OBERON AND PUCK STAND BACK HIDDEN FROM VIEW.

PUCK

(to Oberon) This is the woman, but it's not the man.

DEMETRIUS

Oh, why rebuke the man who loves you so,
Save words so bitter for your bitter foe?

HERMIA

I only scold, though I could say much worse,
For you, I fear, give me much cause to curse.
If you have killed Lysander as he slept,
You're now so drenched in blood, jump in full
*   depth*
And kill me too.
The sun was never more true to each day
Than him to me. Would he have sneaked away
From sleeping Hermia? I'll only believe when
The earth is drilled through and the moon
*   may then*
Creep through the world and come out to
*   displease*
The midday sun in the Antipodes.
It must be so that you have murdered him,
Only a murderer looks so cold and grim.

PUCK

This is the woman, but not this the man.

DEMETRIUS

O, why rebuke you him that loves you so?
Lay breath so bitter on your bitter foe.

HERMIA

Now I but chide; but I should use thee worse,
For thou, I fear, hast given me cause to curse.
If thou hast slain Lysander in his sleep,
Being o'er-shoes in blood, plunge in the deep
And kill me too.
The sun was not so true unto the day
As he to me. Would he have stolen away
From sleeping Hermia? I'll believe as soon
This whole earth may be bored, and that the moon
May through the centre creep, and so displease
Her brother's noontide with th' Antipodes.
It cannot be but thou hast murdered him;
So should a murderer look, so dead, so grim.

Note: 'Antipodes' in this case is Australasia. The point believed to be directly beneath England if you drilled through the earth.

DEMETRIUS

That's how the murdered look, and so should
*   I,*
Pierced through the heart with your stern
*   cruelty.*
But you, my murderer, look bright and clear,
Like Venus, up there in her shimm'ring sphere.

DEMETRIUS

So should the murdered look; and so should I,
Pierced through the heart with your stern cruelty.
Yet you, the murderer, look as bright, as clear,
As yonder Venus in her glimm'ring sphere.

Note: Venus is a planet, but it is known as the evening star, being the first and the brightest 'star' to appear every evening. Again Shakespeare refers to the spheres containing the stars and planets. See Act II, Scene I for more details.

'Cruelty' would have been stressed to rhyme with "I". See note on page 71.

HERMIA

What of my dear Lysander? Where is he?

Please, good Demetrius, give him back to me.

DEMETRIUS

I'd rather feed his body to my hounds.

HERMIA

You dog! You cur! You go beyond the bounds

Of my patience. Have you killed him then?

From now on you'll be lowest among men!

Oh, tell me truly, even for my sake!

Would you have faced him if he'd been awake?

And have you killed him sleeping? What brave touch!

Could even worm or adder do as much?

A snake did it, for with a double tongue

Like yours, you serpent, no snake ever stung

DEMETRIUS

You waste your anger with a misplaced mood.

I've not spilt any of Lysander's blood.

Nor is he dead, as far as I can tell.

HERMIA

I beg you, tell me now that he is well.

DEMETRIUS

And if I could, what would you give me then?

HERMIA

The privilege of seeing me ne'er again.

And from your hated presence I must part

See me no more, whether he is dead or not.

HERMIA

What's this to my Lysander? Where is he?

Ah, good Demetrius, wilt thou give him me?

DEMETRIUS

I had rather give his carcass to my hounds.

HERMIA

Out, dog! Out, cur! Thou driv'st me past the bounds

Of maiden's patience. Hast thou slain him then?

Henceforth be never numbered among men!

O, once tell true, tell true, even for my sake!

Durst thou have looked upon him being awake,

And hast thou killed him sleeping? O brave touch!

Could not a worm, an adder, do so much?

An adder did it; for with doubler tongue

Than thine, thou serpent, never adder stung.

DEMETRIUS

You spend your passion on a misprised mood.

I am not guilty of Lysander's blood;

Nor is he dead, for aught that I can tell.

HERMIA

I pray thee, tell me then that he is well.

DEMETRIUS

An if I could, what should I get therefore.

HERMIA

A privilege never to see me more.

And from thy hated presence part I so.

See me no more, whether he be dead or no.

EXIT HERMIA.

DEMETRIUS

There's no point following her, in this fierce mood.

I'll stay here for a while where I am stood.

The heaviness of sorrow, heavier grows,

From debt of lack of sleep, which sorrow owes,

Which now in small measure it will repay

If for its payment I rest here and stay.

DEMETRIUS

There is no following her in this fierce vein;

Here, therefore, for a while I will remain.

So sorrow's heaviness doth heavier grow

For debt that bankrupt sleep doth sorrow owe,

Which now in some slight measure it will pay,

If for his tender here I make some stay.

Act III Scene II - Another Part Of The Wood.

OBERON

(to Puck)

What have you done? Quite a mistake you've made,

The love juice on the wrong love's eyes you've laid,

From your mistake must certainly ensue

One true-love ended, not false love turned true.

PUCK

Fate over-rules that, one man keeps his troth,

A million more fail, breaking oath on oath.

Note: A troth is a solemn vow, especially in marriage.

OBERON

About the wood go, swifter than the wind,

And Helena of Athens, you must find.

All love-sick that she is and pale of cheek,

Her sighs of love, make her hot blood run weak.

By using magic, see you bring her here.

I'll charm his eyes for when she does appear.

PUCK

I go, I go. Look how I go,

Swift as an arrow from a Tartar's bow.

OBERON

What hast thou done? Thou hast mistaken quite,

And laid the love-juice on some true-love's sight.

Of thy misprision must perforce ensue

Some true-love turned, and not a false turned true.

PUCK

Then fate o'errules, that, one man holding troth,

A million fail, confounding oath on oath.

OBERON

About the wood go swifter than the wind,

And Helena of Athens look thou find.

All fancy-sick she is and pale of cheer,

With sighs of love that costs the fresh blood dear.

By some illusion see thou bring her here;

I'll charm his eyes against she do appear.

PUCK

I go, I go; look how I go,

Swifter than arrow from the Tartar's bow.

Note: Tartars, famed for their archery and cruelty, conquered Asia and Eastern Europe under Genghis Khan in the 13th Century. More correctly they are 'Tatars', but they are commonly known as Tartars. The Tartar Bow was short and light and highly efficient at being fired from horseback while riding.

OBERON

(aside) Flower of this purple hue,
Hit with Cupid's arrow true,
In the centre of its eye.
When its love he does espy,
Let her shine so gloriously
Just like Venus in the sky.
When you wake, if she be near,
Ask her then to be your cure.

OBERON

Flower of this purple dye,
Hit with Cupid's archery,
Sink in apple of his eye.
When his love he doth espy,
Let her shine as gloriously
As the Venus of the sky.
When thou wak'st, if she be by,
Beg of her for remedy.

OBERON SMEARS THE EYES OF DEMETRIUS.

RE-ENTER PUCK.

PUCK

(to Oberon)
Captain of our fairy band
Helena is near at hand,
With the youth, I chose amiss,
Begging for a lover's kiss,
Shall we their love making see?
Lord, what fools these mortals be!

PUCK

Captain of our fairy band,
Helena is here at hand;
And the youth, mistook by me,
Pleading for a lover's fee.
Shall we their fond pageant see?
Lord, what fools these mortals be!

Note: A lover's fee was traditionally three kisses.

'Lord, what fools these mortals be!' is one of the famous quotes from this play.

OBERON

Quickly hide. The noise they make
Will cause Demetrius to wake.

OBERON

Stand aside. The noise they make
Will cause Demetrius to awake.

PUCK

Two of them will then chase one.
This will be the best of fun.
And the things that best please me,
Are those that happen absurdly.

PUCK

Then will two at once woo one.
That must needs be sport alone;
And those things do best please me
That befall preposterously.

THEY STAND ASIDE OUT OF SIGHT.

ENTER LYSANDER AND HELENA.

LYSANDER

Why would you think I mock you with my
  love?
  For true-love never comes with tears of
  scorn.
Look, when I vow I weep, and that does prove,
  I love you, tears are vows from true-love
  born.
How can these tears from me be mocking you,
They are the badge of truth which proves I'm
  true?

HELENA

Your scheming and your talk gets worse and
  worse.
One truth against one truth, how I could
  curse!
Vows meant for Hermia, you'll discard her?
Weigh oath with oath, and both are of no
  worth.
Your vows to her and me, put on two scales,
Will weigh the same and hold no weight,
  they're tales.

LYSANDER

My judgement left me when to her I swore.

HELENA

And more so, in my mind, aband'ning her.

LYSANDER

(*loudly*) Demetrius loves her. He does not
love you.

LYSANDER

Why should you think that I should woo in scorn?
Scorn and derision never come in tears.
Look, when I vow I weep; and vows so born,
In their nativity all truth appears.
How can these things in me seem scorn to you,
Bearing the badge of faith to prove them true?

HELENA

You do advance your cunning more and more.
When truth kills truth, O devilish-holy fray!
These vows are Hermia's. Will you give her o'er?
Weigh oath with oath, and you will nothing weigh.
Your vows to her and me, put in two scales,
Will even weigh; and both as light as tales.

LYSANDER

I had no judgement when to her I swore.

HELENA

Nor none, in my mind, now you give her o'er.

LYSANDER

Demetrius loves her, and he loves not you.

AT THIS DEMETRIUS AWAKES AND SEES HELENA.

HE IS IMMEDIATELY SMITTEN WITH HER.

DEMETRIUS

Oh, Helen! Goddess, nymph, perfect, divine!
My love, to what shall I compare your eyne?
Crystal is murky, oh, how ripe a glow
Comes from your lips, no sweeter cherries
   grow!
The pure white, virginal, mountain's snow,
Cleansed by the eastern wind, looks like a
   crow
(taking her hand in his)
When you hold up your hand. Oh, let me kiss
This princess of pure white, this seal of bliss!

DEMETRIUS

O Helen, goddess, nymph, perfect, divine!
To what, my love, shall I compare thine eyne?
Crystal is muddy. O how ripe in show
Thy lips, those kissing cherries, tempting grow!
That pure congealed white, high Taurus' snow,
Fanned with the eastern wind, turns to a crow
When thou hold'st up thy hand. O let me kiss
This princess of pure white, this seal of bliss!

> Note: 'Taurus' snow' – the Taurus mountain range in southern Turkey.
>
> 'Seal of bliss' – take her hand in marriage, to seal the deal of happiness. A woman's hand was known as a 'white seal of virtue'. Proper ladies would never expose their skin to the sun, so the whiter it was the higher class they were, unblemished hands also showed they never had to work. White was also the colour associated with virginity and marriage. A woman could only get married in white if she was a virgin.

HELENA

Oh spite! Oh hell! I can see you are bent
On ganging against me for your merriment.
If you were noble and knew courtesy
You would not do me this much injury.
Can't you just hate me, as I know you do,
Without joining others to mock me too?
If you were men, like the men you portray,
You'd not treat a humble lady this way.
To vow and swear, and false-praise my parts
When I am sure you hate me in your hearts.
You are both rivals, and love Hermia,
And now those rivals, both mock Helena.
Such fine courage, such manly enterprise,
To make pools of tears in a poor maiden's eyes
With all your mockery! No noble sort
Would so offend a virgin, and extort
A pour maiden's patience, all for your sport.

HELENA

O spite! O hell! I see you are all bent
To set against me for your merriment.
If you were civil and knew courtesy
You would not do me thus much injury.
Can you not hate me, as I know you do,
But you must join in souls to mock me too?
If you were men, as men you are in show,
You would not use a gentle lady so:
To vow, and swear, and superpraise my parts,
When I am sure you hate me with your hearts.
You both are rivals, and love Hermia;
And now both rivals, to mock Helena:
A trim exploit, a manly enterprise,
To conjure tears up in a poor maid's eyes
With your derision! None of noble sort
Would so offend a virgin, and extort
A poor soul's patience, all to make you sport.

> Note: 'Superpraise my parts' – parts means qualities, not individual parts of her. Superpraise is false praise, over the top praise.

LYSANDER

You are unkind, Demetrius. Don't be so,
For you love Hermia, this you know I know.
Here, with all good will, and with all my heart,
For the love of Hermia, I give you my part,
And for yours of Helena to me you'll now give.
Who I now love till I no longer live.

HELENA

Never was mocking with more wasted breath.

DEMETRIUS

Lysander, keep your Hermia, I'll have none.
If I did once love her, all that's now gone.
I gave her my heart as a guest short termed,
And now home to Helen it has returned.
There to remain.

LYSANDER

    Helen, it can't be so.

DEMETRIUS

Don't belittle a faith you do not know,
Or, at your peril you will dearly pay.

LYSANDER

You are unkind, Demetrius. Be not so;
For you love Hermia; this you know I know.
And here, with all good will, with all my heart,
In Hermia's love I yield you up my part;
And yours of Helena to me bequeath,
Whom I do love, and will do till my death.

HELENA

Never did mockers waste more idle breath.

DEMETRIUS

Lysander, keep thy Hermia; I will none.
If e'er I loved her, all that love is gone.
My heart to her but as guestwise sojourned,
And now to Helen is it home returned,
There to remain.

LYSANDER

    Helen, it is not so.

DEMETRIUS

Disparage not the faith thou dost not know,
Lest, to thy peril, thou aby it dear.

RE-ENTER HERMIA.

DEMETRIUS (CONT'D)

Look, over there! See, your love comes this
   way.

HERMIA

Dark night that from the eye its eyesight
   takes,
The ear more sensitive to sound it makes,
But though it does impair the sense of sight,
It doubles the hearing to compensate.
By eye I have not my Lysander found,
My ear, most kindly brought me to your
   sound.
But why unkindly did you leave me so?

DEMETRIUS

Look where thy love comes! Yonder is thy dear.

HERMIA

Dark night that from the eye his function takes,
The ear more quick of apprehension makes;
Wherein it doth impair the seeing sense,
It pays the hearing double recompense.
Thou art not by mine eye, Lysander, found;
Mine ear, I thank it, brought me to thy sound.
But why unkindly didst thou leave me so?

LYSANDER

*Why would he stay when love tempts him to
go?*

HERMIA

*What love could tempt Lysander from my
side?*

LYSANDER

*The love of Lysander's – who now does hide –
Is Helena, whose beauty lights the night
More than the fiery 'o's and eyes of light.
(he points up to the stars)
Why search for me? Would this not let you
know,
The hate I bear you made me leave you so.*

LYSANDER

Why should he stay whom love doth press to go?

HERMIA

What love could press Lysander from my side?

LYSANDER

*Lysander's love - that would not let him bide -
Fair Helena, who more engilds the night
Than all yon fiery oes and eyes of light.
Why seek'st thou me? Could not this make thee know
The hate I bear thee made me leave thee so?*

Note: He puns on the letter 'o' and the letter 'i' – meaning stars being like bright eyes.

HERMIA

*(shocked)
You cannot speak the truth, this cannot be.*

HELENA

*(aside) So! She is in on this conspiracy!
Now I perceive they have conspired all three
To play these tricks of spite to get at me.*

HERMIA

You speak not as you think. It cannot be.

HELENA

*Lo, she is one of this confederacy!
Now I perceive they have conjoined all three
To fashion this false sport in spite of me.*

HELENA TURNS TO FACE HERMIA.

HELENA (CONT'D)

(to Hermia) Hurtful Hermia, most ungrateful woman! Have you conspired? Have you contrived with these two to taunt me with this foul ridicule? Have all the personal secrets that we've both shared, the vows of sisterhood, the hours we spent when we have rued the increasing time that keeps us apart – oh, is all that forgotten? Our school day friendship, the childhood innocence? Us, Hermia, like two creative gods, together with our needles have made one flower, both on one frame, sitting on one cushion, both humming one song, in the same key, as if our hands, our sides, our voices, our minds had been conjoined. We grew up together, like a double cherry on a stalk, seemingly separate but like a whole divided in two. Two lovely berries growing on one stem, with two separate bodies but with one heart. Like coats of arms, with the two halves crowned with a single crest. And you will split our lifelong love apart? To join in with men pouring scorn on your poor friend? It is not friendly, it is not ladylike. Womankind, as well as I, will punish you for it, though I alone feel the hurt.

HELENA

Injurious Hermia, most ungrateful maid!
Have you conspired, have you with these contrived
To bait me with this foul derision?
Is all the counsel that we two have shared,
The sisters' vows, the hours that we have spent
When we have chid the hasty-footed time
For parting us - O, is all forgot?
All schooldays' friendship, childhood innocence?
We, Hermia, like two artificial gods
Have with our needles created both one flower,
Both on one sampler, sitting on one cushion,
Both warbling of one song, both in one key,
As if our hands, our sides, voices, and minds,
Had been incorporate. So we grew together,
Like to a double cherry, seeming parted
But yet a union in partition,
Two lovely berries moulded on one stem;
So, with two seeming bodies but one heart,
Two of the first, like coats in heraldry,
Due but to one, and crowned with one crest.
And will you rent our ancient love asunder,
To join with men in scorning your poor friend?
It is not friendly, 'tis not maidenly;
Our sex, as well as I, may chide you for it,
Though I alone do feel the injury.

Note: In heraldry, a coat of arms could be split into two, often of the two families of both husband and wife, yet it would be crowned on top with a single crest, combined together representing the family. In the example shown here, the coat of arms of Prince Harry and Meghan Markle.

To further his social status, Shakespeare sought a coat of arms for his father. These were finally granted in 1596. Midsummer's Night was written in 1595 or 1596, so not only was the thought fresh in his mind while writing the play, he may have included the reference to promote his quest. This is the coat of arms granted to Shakespeare. A spear with the nib of a pen as the point being shaken by a hawk. Non Sanz Droict means "Not without right" in old French.

83

HERMIA

I am amazed at your passionate words. I do not scorn you. It seems to me that you scorn me.

HELENA

Have you not set up Lysander, to mock me, to follow me and praise my eyes and face? And made your other love, Demetrius, who only a moment ago mocked me by rubbing his foot against mine, calling me his goddess, his nymph, so divine, so rare, such a precious and celestial body? Why would he say this to a woman he hates? And why does Lysander deny his love for you, a love so deep in his soul, and instead give it to me affectionately, if it were not for you setting him on me, with your permission? Why am I not so highly in favour as you, so lovingly embraced, so fortunate, instead I am most miserable to be in love and not be loved back? This should give you reason to pity me, not despise me.

HERMIA

I don't understand what you mean by this.

HELENA

Yes, do - carry on with the pretend serious looks, make mouths at me when I turn my back, wink at each other, keep up the jolly jest. Playing the game so well it will go down in history. If you had any pity, any compassion or manners you would not make me such an object of ridicule. So, goodbye, it's partly my own fault, which death or my leaving will soon rectify.

LYSANDER

Wait, dear Helena, hear me out. My love, my life, my dearest Helena!

HELENA

Oh, great!

HERMIA

I am amazed at your passionate words.
I scorn you not. It seems that you scorn me.

HELENA

Have you not set Lysander, as in scorn,
To follow me and praise my eyes and face?
And made your other love, Demetrius,
Who even but now did spurn me with his foot,
To call me goddess, nymph, divine, and rare,
Precious, celestial? Wherefore speaks he this
To her he hates? And wherefore doth Lysander
Deny your love, so rich within his soul,
And tender me, forsooth, affection,
But by your setting on, by your consent?
What though I be not so in grace as you,
So hung upon with love, so fortunate,
But miserable most, to love unloved?
This you should pity rather than despise.

HERMIA

I understand not what you mean by this.

HELENA

Ay, do - persever, counterfeit sad looks,
Make mouths upon me when I turn my back;
Wink each at other, hold the sweet jest up;
This sport well carried shall be chronicled.
If you have any pity, grace, or manners,
You would not make me such an argument.
But fare ye well: 'tis partly my own fault,
Which death or absence soon shall remedy.

LYSANDER

Stay, gentle Helena; hear my excuse.
My love, my life, my soul, fair Helena!

HELENA

O excellent!

HERMIA (*to Lysander*) Sweetheart, do not mock her so.	HERMIA Sweet, do not scorn her so.
DEMETRIUS If she can't persuade him, I can make him!	DEMETRIUS If she cannot entreat, I can compel.
LYSANDER You can't 'make' me any more than she can 'persuade' me. Your threats have no more effect than her feeble pleading. Helena, I love you, on my life I do. I swear by the life I would willingly sacrifice for you, proving any man wrong who says I do not love you.	LYSANDER Thou canst compel no more than she entreat. Thy threats have no more strength than her weak prayers. Helen, I love thee; by my life, I do. I swear by that which I will lose for thee To prove him false that says I love thee not.
DEMETRIUS (*to Helena*) I say I love you more than he ever could.	DEMETRIUS I say I love thee more than he can do.
LYSANDER You can say it, step with me and prove it too.	LYSANDER If thou say so, withdraw, and prove it too.

LYSANDER INDICATES HIS SWORD, SHOWING HE WISHES TO DUEL.

DEMETRIUS OK, right now, come on.	DEMETRIUS Quick, come.

HERMIA RESTRAINS LYSANDER.

HERMIA Lysander, why are you doing this?	HERMIA Lysander, whereto tends all this?

LYSANDER ATTEMPTS TO SHRUG OFF HERMIA.

LYSANDER Get away, you blackamoor!	LYSANDER Away, you Ethiope!

Note: 'Ethiope' – A dark skinned person in general. Ethiopia is the oldest independent country in Africa. Known of in Shakespeare's time, mainly due to trade and import of workers - not as slaves, a popular misconception. It was a colloquial term for any dark skinned person. Hermia is a Mediterranean woman, dark hair and dark complexion compared to the natural fair complexion of the British. He calls her a 'tawny Tartar' a little further down, another reference to her dark complexion.

DEMETRIUS

(*to Hermia, sarcastically*) Don't worry, he's only pretending to break loose.

(*to Lysander*) Making as if to follow me, but staying where you are. You are a wimp, go away!

LYSANDER

(*to Hermia*) Let go, you hellcat, you thorn! Vile woman, let go, or I will shake you off me like the snake you are.

HERMIA

Why are you so suddenly rude? Why have you changed, dearest love...

LYSANDER

(*interrupting*) Your love! Go, dark savage, go! Away, nauseous medicine! Oh, loathsome poison, go!

DEMETRIUS

No, no; he'll
Seem to break loose -
[*Turning to Lysander*]   take on as you would follow,
But yet come not. You are a tame man, go!

LYSANDER

[*To Hermia.*]
Hang off, thou cat, thou burr! Vile thing, let loose,
Or I will shake thee from me like a serpent!

HERMIA

Why are you grown so rude? What change is this,
Sweet love -

LYSANDER

Thy love! Out, tawny Tartar, out!
Out, loathed med'cine! O hated poison, hence!

HERMIA CONTINUES RESTRAINING LYSANDER, HER ARMS NOW FULLY WRAPPED AROUND HIM.

HELENA THINKS THEY ARE ALL STILL JOKING AT HER EXPENSE.

HERMIA

Surely you are joking?

HELENA

Yes, indeed, and so are you.

LYSANDER

(*still struggling*) Demetrius, I will keep my word on the challenge with you.

DEMETRIUS

(*taunting*) I would rather have your bond, for I see you are easily held by a weak bond. I don't trust your word.

HERMIA

Do you not jest?

HELENA

Yes, sooth, and so do you.

LYSANDER

Demetrius, I will keep my word with thee.

DEMETRIUS

I would I had your bond, for I perceive
A weak bond holds you. I'll not trust your word.

Note: A bond is a legally binding agreement. The 'weak bond' is Hermia's hold on Lysander which he seems unable to break despite being somewhat larger than her.

LYSANDER

What! Do you think I would hurt her, hit her, kill her? I might hate her, but I'll not harm her to escape.

LYSANDER

What, should I hurt her, strike her, kill her dead?
Although I hate her, I'll not harm her so.

HERMIA

What? You think you can do me greater harm than hating me? You hate me?! For what reason? Oh my, that is unexpected news, my love! Am I not still Hermia? Are you not still Lysander? I am still as beautiful as I was before. Last night you loved me, yet since last night you've left me. That means, you are saying – oh, god forbid! – that you really do mean to leave me?

LYSANDER

Yes. On my life. And I never want to see you again. So give up hope. Don't question or doubt me, nothing could be more certain, not a truer word spoken. It's not a joke that I hate you and love Helena.

HERMIA

Oh, my!
(*to Helena*) You cheat, Helena, you diseased flower, you thief of love! What? Did you come here tonight to steal my love's heart away from him?

HELENA

Fine indeed! Have you no modesty, Hermia, no womanly shame, no hint of bashfulness? What? You try to provoke harsh answers from my gentle tongue? Fie, fie! You fake, you puppet, you!

HERMIA

Puppet? How so? Ah, so that's how the game works. Now I see, she's making comparisons about our height. She is boasting about her height, and her figure, her tall figure, she has seduced him with her height, no less. And have you grown so high in his esteem because I am so short and so low? How low am I, you painted flagpole? Answer me. How low am I? I am not so low that my nails can't reach up to your eyes!

HERMIA

What, can you do me greater harm than hate?
Hate me! Wherefore? O me, what news, my love!
Am not I Hermia? Are not you Lysander?
I am as fair now as I was erewhile.
Since night you loved me; yet since night you left
  me.
Why then, you left me - O the gods forbid! -
In earnest, shall I say?

LYSANDER

Ay, by my life;
And never did desire to see thee more.
Therefore be out of hope, of question, of doubt;
Be certain, nothing truer; 'tis no jest
That I do hate thee and love Helena.

HERMIA

O me, you juggler, you canker-blossom,
You thief of love! What, have you come by night
And stol'n my love's heart from him?

HELENA

Fine, i'faith!
Have you no modesty, no maiden shame,
No touch of bashfulness? What, will you tear
Impatient answers from my gentle tongue?
Fie, fie, you counterfeit, you puppet, you!

HERMIA

Puppet? Why so? Ay, that way goes the game.
Now I perceive that she hath made compare
Between our statures. She hath urged her height,
And with her personage, her tall personage,
Her height, forsooth, she hath prevailed with him.
And are you grown so high in his esteem
Because I am so dwarfish and so low?
How low am I, thou painted maypole? Speak;
How low am I? I am not yet so low
But that my nails can reach unto thine eyes.

HERMIA RELEASES LYSANDER AND MAKES TOWARDS HELENA. DEMETRIUS PREVENTS HER. HELENA IS NOW FRIGHTENED AND HIDES BEHIND DEMETRIUS.

HELENA

Though you mock me, gentlemen, I beg you, do not let her hurt me. I was never spiteful, I am not in the slightest way a shrew. I am a typical woman in my cowardice. Don't let her hit me. Even though you may think that because she is shorter than me I am a match for her.

HELENA

I pray you, though you mock me, gentlemen,
Let her not hurt me. I was never curst;
I have no gift at all in shrewishness;
I am a right maid for my cowardice.
Let her not strike me. You perhaps may think,
Because she is something lower than myself,
That I can match her.

Note: A shrew is a bad tempered woman.

HERMIA

Shorter! Here we go again.

HERMIA

Lower! Hark, again.

HELENA

Good, Hermia, don't be so bitter with me. I've always loved you, Hermia. I've always kept your secrets, I've never wronged you, except for what I did out of love for Demetrius. I told him about you secretly fleeing to this wood. He followed you. Out of love I followed him. But he has chastised me, and threatened to strike me, to reject me, no, even so far as to kill me. And now, if you'll let me go quietly back to Athens I will carry my foolish self back, and follow you no more. Let me go, you can see how naïve and simple I am.

HELENA

Good Hermia, do not be so bitter with me.
I evermore did love you, Hermia;
Did ever keep your counsels, never wronged you,
Save that in love unto Demetrius
I told him of your stealth into this wood.
He followed you; for love I followed him;
But he hath chid me hence, and threatened me
To strike me, spurn me, nay, to kill me too.
And now, so you will let me quiet go,
To Athens will I bear my folly back,
And follow you no further. Let me go;
You see how simple and how fond I am.

HERMIA

Well, go away then. What is stopping you?

HERMIA

Why, get you gone. Who is't that hinders you?

HELENA

A foolish heart, that I leave behind here.

HELENA

A foolish heart, that I leave here behind.

HERMIA

(angry) What? With Lysander?

HERMIA

What, with Lysander?

HELENA

With Demetrius.

HELENA

With Demetrius.

LYSANDER

Don't be afraid. She'll not harm you, Helena.

LYSANDER

Be not afraid; she shall not harm thee, Helena.

DEMETRIUS

No, sir, she will not, though you take her side.

HELENA

Oh, when she's angry she is cunning and shrewd. She was a vixen when she was at school, and though she is only little, she is fierce.

DEMETRIUS

No, sir, she shall not, though you take her part.

HELENA

O, when she's angry she is keen and shrewd.
She was a vixen when she went to school,
And, though she is but little, she is fierce.

Note: 'Vixen' – a female fox, an animal noted for its cunning.

HERMIA

Little again! Nothing but short and little! Why do you allow her to insult me like this? Let me at her!

HERMIA

Little again! Nothing but low and little!
Why will you suffer her to flout me thus?
Let me come to her.

HERMIA LUNGES FOR HELENA. DEMETRIUS PREVENTS HER.

LYSANDER

(to Hermia) Get out of here, you dwarf, you midget, bound in reeds to prevent growth, you fairy, you acorn!

DEMETRIUS

(to Lysander) You are overly supportive of her that mocks your offers. Leave Hermia alone. And don't speak about Helena. You don't speak on her behalf, and if you intend to show even the smallest bit of love towards her, you will pay dearly.

LYSANDER

She's no longer holding me back.
Now, follow me, if you dare, we'll settle who has the greatest right to Helena, you or I.

DEMETRIUS

Follow! No, I'll walk with you side by side.

LYSANDER

Get you gone, you dwarf,
You minimus, of hind'ring knot-grass made;
You bead, you acorn.

DEMETRIUS

You are too officious
In her behalf that scorns your services.
Let her alone. Speak not of Helena;
Take not her part; for if thou dost intend
Never so little show of love to her,
Thou shalt aby it.

LYSANDER

Now she holds me not.
Now follow, if thou dar'st, to try whose right,
Of thine or mine, is most in Helena.

DEMETRIUS

Follow! Nay, I'll go with thee cheek by jowl.

Note: 'Cheek by jowl' is a expression which had been around centuries before Shakespeare. The similar expression 'cheek to cheek' is used to describe a close, romantic situation, whereas 'cheek by jowl' suggests the opposite, a cramped, crowded, aggressive situation.

EXEUNT LYSANDER AND DEMETRIUS DEFIANTLY.

HERMIA MOVES TOWARDS HELENA THREATENINGLY.

HERMIA
And you, madam, all this trouble has been caused by you.

HERMIA
You, mistress, all this coil is 'long of you.

HELENA BACKS AWAY, FRIGHTENED.

HERMIA (CONT'D)
No, don't back away.

HERMIA
Nay, go not back.

HELENA
I don't trust you, I don't. Nor will I stay any longer in your cursed company.
Your hands are quicker at starting a fray,
My legs are longer, so I'll run away.

HELENA
I will not trust you, I,
Nor longer stay in your curst company.
Your hands than mine are quicker for a fray;
My legs are longer, though, to run away.

EXIT HELENA.

HERMIA
I am amazed and don't know what to say.

HERMIA
I am amazed, and know not what to say.

EXIT HERMIA FOLLOWING AFTER HELENA.

OBERON ADVANCES WITH PUCK FROM THEIR HIDING PLACE.

OBERON
This is a result of your negligence. You are either making yet more mistakes or this is a deliberate act of mischief.

OBERON
This is thy negligence. Still thou mistak'st,
Or else committ'st thy knaveries wilfully.

PUCK
Believe me, King of shadows, I was mistaken.
Did you not tell me I would know the man
By the Athenian garments he had on?
And so I'm blameless in this enterprise
For I have charmed an Athenian's eyes.
So far I'm glad that it happened this way,
As their rows and fighting I hold in much sway.

PUCK
Believe me, King of shadows, I mistook.
Did not you tell me I should know the man
By the Athenian garments he had on?
And so far blameless proves my enterprise
That I have 'nointed an Athenian's eyes;
And so far am I glad it did so sort,
As this their jangling I esteem a sport.

Note: 'King of shadows' – shadowy beings, meaning the fairies.

Act III Scene II - Another Part Of The Wood.

OBERON

You've seen these lovers seek a place to fight.
Go therefore, Robin, cloud over the night.
The starry night sky, cover it soon
With a hanging fog black as Acheron.

OBERON

Thou seest these lovers seek a place to fight.
Hie therefore, Robin, overcast the night;
The starry welkin cover thou anon
With drooping fog as black as Acheron,

[handwritten:] step 1 make it so they can't see

Note: 'Welkin' – Sky.

'Acheron' – One of the rivers of Hades in mythology, a river in hell.

OBERON (CONT'D)

And lead these angry rivals so astray
That one does not pass by another's way.
Sound like Lysander and speak in false
* tongues,*
To anger Demetrius with some bitter wrongs,
And be like Demetrius, call oaths and shout,
And by these means you will lead them apart.
Till death-like sleep to their eyes it does crawl,
With lead-like legs, fluttering eyelids fall.

OBERON

And lead these testy rivals so astray
As one come not within another's way.
Like to Lysander sometime frame thy tongue,
Then stir Demetrius up with bitter wrong;
And sometime rail thou like Demetrius;
And from each other look thou lead them thus,
Till o'er their brows death-counterfeiting sleep
With leaden legs and batty wings doth creep.

[handwritten:] step 2 don't have them fight

[handwritten:] step 3 make them fall asleep

OBERON PASSES A VIAL TO PUCK.

Note: In the next line, Oberon says 'crush this herb' which makes it sound like the flower is being squeezed, in which case he would pass Puck some kind of plant. But productions often use a vial (or phial) of liquid. (Phial and vial are much the same thing, both are glass containers, typically for medicines).

OBERON (CONT'D)

Then crush this herb into Lysander's eye,
Whose liquid has a mighty property,
To take from them all error of this night
And make his eyeballs see with normal sight.
When they next wake, all of this deception
Will seem like a dream, an empty vision.
And back to Athens the lovers shall head
And be friends again until their death-bed.
While in this affair I do you employ,
I'll beg my queen for her Indian boy.
And then her bewitched eye I will release
From monster's love and things will be in
* peace.*

OBERON

Then crush this herb into Lysander's eye;
Whose liquor hath this virtuous property,
To take from thence all error with his might
And make his eyeballs roll with wonted sight.
When they next wake, all this derision
Shall seem a dream and fruitless vision;
And back to Athens shall the lovers wend
With league whose date till death shall never end.
Whiles I in this affair do thee employ,
I'll to my queen and beg her Indian boy;
And then I will her charmed eye release
From monster's view, and all things shall be peace.

[handwritten:] step 3 put onto Lysander's eye

[handwritten:] step 4

91

PUCK

My fairy lord, this has to be done soon,
For night-time's dragons will block out the
moon.
Over there shines Aurora's morning star,
When it appears ghosts who walked near and
far,
Troop home to graves. Except damned spirits
all,
Who at crossroads and floods had burial,
Already to their wormy beds have gone,
For fear of shame which day looks down upon
They purposely hide themselves from daylight,
Their company forever black-faced night.

PUCK

My fairy lord, this must be done with haste,
For night's swift dragons cut the clouds full fast,
And yonder shines Aurora's harbinger,
At whose approach ghosts, wand'ring here and there,
Troop home to churchyards. Damned spirits all,
That in crossways and floods have burial,
Already to their wormy beds are gone,
For fear lest day should look their shames upon;
They wilfully themselves exile from light,
And must for aye consort with black-browed night.

> Note: 'Dragons' – like the steeds that pulled the sun chariot of day, dragons were said to pull over the blanket of night.
>
> Aurora is the goddess of dawn. Cephalus was her lover, referred to in the next speech by Oberon as "morning's love".
>
> 'Crossways and floods have burial' – suicides were buried at crossroads so their graves were trampled on by all instead of being sacred in a graveyard. The ghosts of those who drowned were condemned to wander the earth for one-hundred years because they did not receive the religious rites of burial.

OBERON

But we are spirits of another sort.
I have with Cephalus often made sport,
And like a forester may tread the woods
Until the eastern sky in fiery reds
Lights up Neptune's waves with sun blessed
beams,
Turning golden his salted green streams.
But even so, make haste and not delay,
We still can end this business 'fore it's day.

OBERON

But we are spirits of another sort.
I with the morning's love have oft made sport,
And like a forester the groves may tread
Even till the eastern gate, all fiery red,
Opening on Neptune with fair blessed beams,
Turns into yellow gold his salt green streams.
But, notwithstanding, haste; make no delay;
We may effect this business yet ere day.

> Note: "Morning's love" - Cephalus was the lover of the dawn goddess, Aurora. Oberon cavorts with him before daybreak, so Oberon is not one of the spirits that have to eternally walk the night and go back to their grave by daylight.

EXIT OBERON.

Act III Scene II - Another Part Of The Wood.

PUCK

Up and down, up and down,
I will lead them up and down.
I am feared in fields and town.
Puck will lead them up and down.
- Here comes one.

PUCK

Up and down, up and down,
I will lead them up and down.
I am feared in field and town.
Goblin, lead them up and down.
Here comes one.

Note: 'Goblin' – Puck is a goblin, a mischievous sprite.

RE-ENTER LYSANDER.

LYSANDER

Where are you, vain Demetrius? Speak up, do.

LYSANDER

Where art thou, proud Demetrius? Speak thou now.

PUCK

(imitating Demetrius)
Here, villain, drawn and ready. Where are
you?

PUCK

[*Imitating Demetrius.*]
Here, villain; drawn and ready. Where art thou?

Note: 'Drawn and ready' – with his sword drawn (out) and ready to be used.

LYSANDER

I'll be right with you.

LYSANDER

I will be with thee straight.

PUCK

(imitating Demetrius)
Follow me, then, to open ground.

PUCK

[*Imitating Demetrius.*]
Follow me, then,
To plainer ground.

EXIT LYSANDER, FOLLOWING THE VOICE.

RE-ENTER DEMETRIUS.

DEMETRIUS

Lysander, speak again!
You runaway, you coward, have you fled?
Speak! Is it some bush where you hide your
head?

DEMETRIUS

Lysander, speak again!
Thou runaway, thou coward, art thou fled?
Speak! In some bush? Where dost thou hide thy head?

DEMETRIUS POKES AT RANDOM BUSHES WITH HIS SWORD.

PUCK

(imitating Lysander)

You coward, are you bragging to the stars?

Telling the bushes you're looking for wars?

You won't come out? Come out, rogue. Come
out, child.

I'll thrash you with a rod. He is defiled

Who draws a sword on you.

DEMETRIUS

Hey, are you there?

PUCK

(imitating Lysander)

Follow my voice, we'll not test manhood here.

PUCK

[*Imitating Lysander.*]

Thou coward, art thou bragging to the stars,

Telling the bushes that thou look'st for wars,

And wilt not come? Come, recreant; come, thou child.

I'll whip thee with a rod; he is defiled

That draws a sword on thee.

DEMETRIUS

Yea, art thou there?

PUCK

[*Imitating Lysander.*]

Follow my voice; we'll try no manhood here.

EXIT DEMETRIUS AND PUCK.

RE-ENTER LYSANDER.

LYSANDER

He dares me and yet he's still walking on.

When I get where he called, then he is gone.

The villain is lighter of foot than me.

I followed fast, but faster did he flee.

The ground here now has dark and bumpy
lay,

So here I'll rest, until the gentle day.

LYSANDER

He goes before me, and still dares me on.

When I come where he calls, then he is gone.

The villain is much lighter-heeled than I.

I followed fast, but faster did he fly;

That fallen am I in dark uneven way,

And here will rest me. Come, thou gentle day;

LYSANDER LIES DOWN.

LYSANDER (CONT'D)

As soon as it shows me its new grey light,

I'll find Demetrius, and settle this fight.

LYSANDER

For if but once thou show me thy grey light,

I'll find Demetrius, and revenge this spite.

LYSANDER SLEEPS.

RE-ENTER PUCK AND DEMETRIUS.

PUCK

(imitating Lysander)

Come on, you coward, why don't you come
here?

PUCK

[*Imitating Lysander.*]

Ho, ho, ho, coward; why com'st thou not?

DEMETRIUS

Wait for me, if you dare, for well I fear,
You're running ahead, all over the place,
And dare not stop and look me in the face.
Where are you now?

PUCK

(imitating Lysander)
                    Come this way. I am here.

DEMETRIUS

No, now you mock me. You'll pay for this dear
If ever in daylight your face I see.
Now, go away. Faintness overcomes me
So I'll lay down here upon this cold bed.
At daybreak, expect to be visited.

DEMETRIUS

Abide me, if thou dar'st; for well I wot
Thou runn'st before me, shifting every place,
And dar'st not stand nor look me in the face.
Where art thou now?

PUCK

[Imitating Lysander.]
                    Come hither; I am here.

DEMETRIUS

Nay, then thou mock'st me. Thou shalt buy this dear
If ever I thy face by daylight see.
Now, go thy way. Faintness constraineth me
To measure out my length on this cold bed.
By day's approach look to be visited.

DEMETRIUS LIES DOWN AND SLEEPS.

RE-ENTER HELENA.

HELENA

Oh, weary night, oh long and tiring night,
  Shorten your hours, shine comfort from the
  east
So I can head back to Athens in light,
  Away from those who my presence detest.
And sleep, that shuts out sorrow from my eye,
Take me away from my own company.

HELENA

O weary night, O long and tedious night,
  Abate thy hours, shine comforts from the east
That I may back to Athens by daylight,
  From these that my poor company detest.
And sleep, that sometimes shuts up sorrow's eye,
Steal me awhile from mine own company.

Note: See note on the rhyming of 'eye' with 'company' on page 71.

HELENA LIES DOWN AND SLEEPS.

PUCK

Only three? Come one more,
Two of both sex makes up four.
Here she comes, cross and sad.
Cupid is a naughty lad
To make such poor females mad.

PUCK

Yet but three? Come one more;
Two of both kinds makes up four.
Here she comes, curst and sad.
Cupid is a knavish lad
Thus to make poor females mad.

RE-ENTER HERMIA.

HERMIA

Never so weary, and so full of woe.
  All soaking from the dew, and torn with
  briars,
I can no farther crawl, no farther go.
  My legs can't keep pace with my mind's
  desires.
Here I will rest until the break of day.
Heaven, help Lysander if they start a fray!

HERMIA

Never so weary, never so in woe;
  Be dabbled with the dew, and torn with briars;
I can no further crawl, no further go;
  My legs can keep no pace with my desires.
Here will I rest me till the break of day.
Heavens, shield Lysander if they mean a fray!

HERMIA LIES DOWN AND SLEEPS.

PUCK

On the ground
Sleeping sound.
I'll apply
  To your eye,
Gentle love's sweet remedy.

PUCK

On the ground
Sleep sound.
I'll apply
  To your eye,
Gentle lover, remedy.

PUCK SQUEEZES THE JUICE ON LYSANDER'S EYES.

PUCK (CONT'D)

When you wake
You will take
True delight
In the sight
Of your former lover's eye.
And the old proverb, well known,
That everyman should take his own,
As you wake up shall be shown.
  Jack shall have Jill.
  None shall go ill.
The man shall have his mare again, and all
  shall be well.

PUCK

When thou wak'st
Thou tak'st
True delight
In the sight
Of thy former lady's eye;
And the country proverb known,
That every man should take his own,
In your waking shall be shown:
  Jack shall have Jill,
  Naught shall go ill;
The man shall have his mare again, and all shall be well.

> Note: 'Every man should take his own' – the woman for him. Somewhere there is a woman compatible for every man. Puck is putting the correct pairs together again.
>
> Jack and Jill were common names for simple country couples and often used in early literature. A common saying of the time was 'Every Jack shall have his Jill', meaning every man will find a compatible woman. The famous Jack and Jill nursery rhyme would not come about for almost 200 years after Shakespeare wrote this play. 'Jack and Jill fell down the hill' was based on the beheadings of Louis XVI and his wife Marie Antoinette. The language was sweetened so children could sing it.
>
> A 'mare' is a female horse. Slang for 'woman'.

Act III Scene II - Another Part Of The Wood.

Trivia: The nursery rhyme most English children learn explained;

Jack and Jill fell down the hill - Louis and Marie's reign came tumbling down for them.

Jack broke his crown – he lost his royal crown and his head, which crown also means.

And Jill came tumbling after – Marie was beheaded after Louis.

The sweetened ending is 'Up Jack got, and home did trot, as fast as he could caper, he went to bed and wrapped his head in vinegar and brown paper' - Obviously he couldn't mend his head but it is thought this alluded to the fact that the head stayed alive for some seconds after death and was held up by the hair, not to be shown to the crowd, but for the head to see the crowd cheering and its own body lying separate. Gory stuff.

EXIT PUCK LEAVING THE FOUR LOVERS ASLEEP.

ACT IV

ATHENS

A WOOD NEAR ATHENS

AND KISS THY FAIR LARGE EARS, MY GENTLE JOY

ACT IV

ACT IV SCENE I

ANOTHER PART OF THE WOOD, LATER ON.

LYSANDER, DEMETRIUS, HELENA, AND HERMIA ARE LYING ASLEEP.

ENTER QUEEN OF THE FAIRIES, (TITANIA) WITH THE CLOWN, (BOTTOM WEARING AN ASS'S HEAD).

ENTER FAIRIES, PEASEBLOSSOM, COBWEB, MOTH, MUSTARDSEED, AND OTHER FAIRIES ATTENDING TITANIA.

ENTER KING OF THE FAIRIES, (OBERON) BEHIND THEM, INVISIBLE.

TITANIA
Come sit down here on this flowery bed,
While I your lovable cheeks do stroke.
And stick sweet roses in your sleek smooth head,
And with gentle kiss, joy to your ears make.

BOTTOM
(*pretentious accent*)
Where's Peaseblossom?

PEASEBLOSSOM
Ready.

BOTTOM
Scratch my head, Peaseblossom. Where's Monsieur Cobweb?

COBWEB
Ready.

BOTTOM
Monsieur Cobweb, good monsieur, go get your weapons in your hand and kill me that red-hipped bumble bee on top of the thistle. And, good monsieur, bring me back the honey bag.

TITANIA
Come, sit thee down upon this flowery bed,
While I thy amiable cheeks do coy,
And stick musk-roses in thy sleek smooth head,
And kiss thy fair large ears, my gentle joy.

BOTTOM
Where's Peaseblossom?

PEASEBLOSSOM
Ready.

BOTTOM
Scratch my head, Peaseblossom. Where's mounsieur Cobweb?

COBWEB
Ready.

BOTTOM
Mounsieur Cobweb, good mounsieur, get you your weapons in your hand and kill me a red-hipped humble-bee on the top of a thistle; and, good mounsieur, bring me the honey-bag.

AS COBWEB LEAVES BOTTOM CALLS AFTER HIM.

BOTTOM (CONT'D)
Do not exert yourself overly in getting it, monsieur, and, good monsieur, take care not to break the honey bag, I would hate that you should get covered with honey, signor.
Where's Monsieur Mustardseed?

BOTTOM
Do not fret yourself too much in the action, mounsieur; and, good mounsieur, have a care the honey-bag break not; I would be loath to have you overflowen with a honey-bag, signor. Where's Mounsieur Mustardseed?

MUSTARDSEED
Ready.

MUSTARDSEED
Ready.

MUSTARDSEED BOWS TO BOTTOM.

BOTTOM
Give me your hand, Monsieur Mustardseed, I insist, there is no need to bow, good monsieur.

BOTTOM
Give me your neaf, Mounsieur Mustardseed. Pray you, leave your courtesy, good mounsieur.

MUSTARDSEED
What is your desire?

MUSTARDSEED
What's your will?

BOTTOM
Nothing more, good monsieur, than to help Cavalier Cobweb to scratch me. I must go to the barber's, monsieur, for I believe I am excessively hairy on my face, and I am such a tender ass that if my hair tickles me I must scratch.

BOTTOM
Nothing, good mounsieur, but to help Cavalery Cobweb to scratch. I must go to the barber's, mounsieur, for methinks I am marvellous hairy about the face; and I am such a tender ass, if my hair do but tickle me I must scratch.

PEASEBLOSSOM REACTS AT BEING CONFUSED WITH COBWEB, WHO IS COLLECTING HONEY BAGS FOR BOTTOM.

Note: It was not Cobweb who was asked to scratch his head, it was Peaseblossom. Another confused uttering from Bottom.

Barber – A man who cuts men's hair and beards, (and performed surgery in the days when medical practises were primitive, such as blood letting, amputations and tooth extractions). Dating back to Roman Times, barber's shops still to this day have the red and white (sometimes now with blue) barber's pole outside which originally signified surgery was available on the premises.

The wordplay on ass for donkey and backside is deliberate. It will be appreciated by the American readers more as the word 'ass' is used for backside there. In the UK the word 'arse' is used. Ass also means a fool.

TITANIA

Now, would you like some music, my sweet love?

TITANIA

What, wilt thou hear some music, my sweet love?

BOTTOM

I have a *reasonable* good ear in music. Let's have the wooden tongs and the bone clappers.

BOTTOM

I have a reasonable good ear in music. Let's have the tongs and the bones.

> Note: 'Tongs and bones' - wooden tongs are struck like a triangle, bones are clicked together like clappers.
>
> Bottom is a weaver, weavers were famed for their singing as they worked, keeping the rhythm of their work.

RURAL MUSIC PLAYS, WITH TONGS AND BONES.

TITANIA

Or tell me, sweet love, what you desire to eat.

TITANIA

Or say, sweet love, what thou desir'st to eat.

BOTTOM

Truly, a lot of fodder, I could munch on your good dry *oats*. I think I also have a desire for a *bottle* of hay. Good hay, sweet hay, has no equal.

BOTTOM

Truly, a peck of provender; I could munch your good dry oats. Methinks I have a great desire to a bottle of hay. Good hay, sweet hay, hath no fellow.

> Note: A 'peck' is an old term for a large amount, and also a measure of dried goods. A 'Peck' was a quarter of a Bushel, or two imperial gallons (nine litres), and used most commonly for measuring horse feed. Famously used in the tongue-twister 'Peter Piper picked a peck of pickled peppers'.
>
> 'Provender' is dry food for animals, hay, corn, oats etc.
>
> 'Oats' was probably an innuendo, from 'getting your oats' – having sex, originally from the expression 'sowing your wild oats' which was for a man to have sex indiscriminately, typically before getting married and settling down to one woman. As men demanded the wife be a virgin, maths suggests a lot of men were fooled.
>
> 'Bottle' – of course, hay doesn't come in bottles, this was another Bottom blunder, though Shakespeare was cleverly playing on the term 'botte' which was a bundle of hay.

TITANIA

I have a brave fairy who shall seek out the squirrel's hoard, and fetch you fresh nuts.

TITANIA

I have a venturous fairy that shall seek The squirrel's hoard, and fetch thee new nuts.

> Note: 'Venturous' – brave, because squirrels are ferociously protective. Squirrels famously hoard nuts away by burying them for winter, but they also famously often forget where they have hidden them.

BOTTOM

I would rather have a handful or two of dried peas. But, I beg you, let none of your people disturb me, I have an *exposition* of sleep come across me.

BOTTOM

I had rather have a handful or two of dried pease. But, I pray you, let none of your people stir me; I have an exposition of sleep come upon me.

> Note: 'Exposition' is again a word Bottom is using to sound educated but gets wrong. He means a disposition, an inclination or an urge towards something. An exposition is a public display of something.

TITANIA

You sleep, I will wrap you in my arms.
(*to Fairies*) Fairies, be gone, do your tasks elsewhere.

TITANIA

Sleep thou, and I will wind thee in my arms.
Fairies, be gone, and be all ways away.

EXEUNT FAIRIES EXCEPT TITANIA.

TITANIA WRAPS HER ARMS AROUND BOTTOM LOVINGLY.

TITANIA (CONT'D)

(*to Bottom, gently*) Just like the woodbine and the honeysuckle gently entwine, and the female ivy surrounds the barky fingers of the elm. Oh, how I love you! How I dote on you!

TITANIA

So doth the woodbine the sweet honeysuckle
Gently entwist; the female ivy so
Enrings the barky fingers of the elm.
O, how I love thee! How I dote on thee!

> Note: Sexual innuendos when said softly and sensuously.

TITANIA AND BOTTOM SLEEP. PUCK ENTERS.

UPON SEEING PUCK, OBERON ADVANCES.

OBERON

Greetings, good Robin. Do you see this sweet sight? I am beginning to take pity on her infatuation now. When I met her a short while ago behind the wood collecting sweet bouquets for this despicable fool, I scolded her, and had a big row with her, for she adorned his hairy head with garlands and bouquets of fresh fragrant flowers, and the dew drops which appear on morning buds, swelling like round glowing pearls, hung from the pretty flower's eyes, like tears of sadness at their own disgrace.

OBERON

Welcome, good Robin. Seest thou this sweet sight?
Her dotage now I do begin to pity,
For, meeting her of late behind the wood
Seeking sweet favours for this hateful fool,
I did upbraid her and fall out with her;
For she his hairy temples then had rounded
With coronet of fresh and fragrant flowers;
And that same dew which sometime on the buds
Was wont to swell like round and orient pearls
Stood now within the pretty flowerets' eyes,
Like tears that did their own disgrace bewail.

Note: 'Temples' – a clever pun on words, his head and the temple which she worships.
'Orient' – bright, the light coming from the East, the direction of the Orient.

OBERON

When I was done with taunting her, and she had politely begged me not to be angry with her, I asked her for the changeling child, which she gave to me straight away, and sent her fairy to carry him to my dwelling in Fairyland. Now that I have the boy I will undo the spell which distorts her vision so horribly. And, gentle Puck, take this alternative skin from the head of this Athenian labourer, so that when he, and the others awake, they can all return to Athens and think of tonight's incidents as nothing more than the wild imaginings of a dream. But first I must uncharm the Fairy Queen.

OBERON

When I had at my pleasure taunted her,
And she in mild terms begged my patience,
I then did ask of her her changeling child;
Which straight she gave me, and her fairy sent
To bear him to my bower in Fairyland.
And now I have the boy I will undo
This hateful imperfection of her eyes.
And, gentle Puck, take this transformed scalp
From of the head of this Athenian swain
That he, awaking when the other do,
May all to Athens back again repair,
And think no more of this night's accidents
But as the fierce vexation of a dream.
But first I will release the Fairy Queen.

OBERON SQUEEZES JUICE ON THE SLEEPING TITANIA'S EYES.

Act IV Scene I - Another Part Of The Wood, Later On.

OBERON	OBERON
Be as you before have been	*Be as thou wast wont to be;*
See as you before have seen	*See as thou wast wont to see.*
Chastity verses Cupid's flower	*Dian's bud o'er Cupid's flower*
Has such force and blessed power	*Hath such force and blessed power.*
Now, my Titania, awake, my sweet queen.	*Now, my Titania, wake you; my sweet queen.*

> Note: 'Dian's' – Diana, goddess of chastity and of the moon. Cupid represents love,
> the opposite of Diana.

TITANIA WAKES UP AND SEES OBERON.

TITANIA	TITANIA
My Oberon, what visions I have seen!	*My Oberon, what visions have I seen!*
I thought I'd fallen in love with an ass.	*Methought I was enamoured of an ass.*
OBERON	OBERON
Your love lies there.	*There lies your love.*
TITANIA	TITANIA
How did this come to pass?	*How came these things to pass?*
Oh, how my eyes hate his face now!	*O how mine eyes do loathe his visage now!*
OBERON	OBERON
All in good time. - Robin, take off his head.	*Silence awhile. Robin, take off this head.*
-Titania, call for music and make more dead	*Titania, music call, and strike more dead*
All these five than with normal sleep.	*Than common sleep of all these five the sense.*
TITANIA	TITANIA
Fairies, music! To charm them all to sleep.	*Music, ho! Music such as charmeth sleep.*

THE FAIRIES PLAY SOFT MUSIC.

PUCK REMOVES THE ASS'S HEAD WITH A SPELL.

PUCK	PUCK
When you awake through your own fool's eyes peep.	*Now, when thou wak'st with thine own fool's eyes peep.*
OBERON	OBERON
Dance, music!	*Sound, music!*

FASTER MUSIC PLAYS. OBERON OFFERS HIS HAND TO TITANIA AS IF FOR A
DANCE.

OBERON (CONT'D)

Come, my queen, take hands with me,
And rock the ground here where these
sleepers be.

OBERON

Come, my queen, take hands with me,
And rock the ground whereon these sleepers be.

Note: 'Rock the ground' – not rock and roll, this is in the sense of rock the cradle.

OBERON AND TITANIA DANCE.

OBERON (CONT'D)

Now you and I are new friends once again,
Midnight tomorrow we'll dance a refrain
In Duke Theseus' house triumphantly,
And bless it with greatest prosperity.
There shall two pairs of faithful lovers be
Married with Theseus, in all jollity.

OBERON

Now thou and I are new in amity,
And will tomorrow midnight solemnly
Dance in Duke Theseus' house triumphantly,
And bless it to all fair prosperity.
There shall the pairs of faithful lovers be
Wedded, with Theseus, all in jollity.

PUCK

Fairy king, take note, and hark,
I can hear the morning lark.

PUCK

Fairy king, attend, and mark;
I do hear the morning lark.

Note: The lark, the herald of the morning, was one of the first birds to sing at dawn as the sun started to rise. Shakespeare mentions it often to signify morning, most famously in Romeo and Juliet for the parting lovers.

OBERON

Then, my queen, in sober silence
We will follow night time's presence
We can travel around the globe,
Swifter than the moon's glowing orb.

OBERON

Then, my queen, in silence sad
Trip we after night's shade.
We the globe can compass soon,
Swifter than the wand'ring moon.

TITANIA

Come, my lord, and in our flight
Tell me what occurred last night
That I asleep right here was found
With these mortals on the ground.

TITANIA

Come, my lord, and in our flight
Tell me how it came this night
That I sleeping here was found
With these mortals on the ground.

OBERON AND TITANIA FLY AWAY TO CHASE THE NIGHT, LEAVING THE FOUR
LOVERS AND BOTTOM ASLEEP.

A HORN BLOWS IN THE DISTANCE.

ENTER THESEUS, HIPPOLYTA, EGEUS AND ATTENDANTS.

THESEUS

Go, one of you, find the huntsman, for now we have performed our rites to this May Day morning, and since we have the day before us, my love, Hippolyta, shall hear the music of my hounds. Release them in the western valley, let them run. Hurry now, and find the huntsman.

THESEUS

Go, one of you, find out the forester;
For now our observation is performed,
And since we have the the vaward of the day,
My love shall hear the music of my hounds.
Uncouple in the western valley; let them go.
Dispatch, I say, and find the forester.

> Note: Shakespeare has the time as May Day in the play, but the title of the play says 'Midsummer' which takes place between June 19th to 24th. Even with the confusion of the changing of calendars in 1582 while Shakespeare was alive, midsummer was never in May. (his first play was probably written in or after 1589). Both Midsummer's Night and May Day were celebrated, Midsummer particularly being associated with supernatural beings and happenings.
>
> We know the 'observation' Theseus talks of was the performing of the Rites of May because Lysander tells us this back in Act I, Scene I.

EXIT AN ATTENDANT.

THESEUS (CONT'D)

My beautiful queen, we'll climb to the mountain's top,
And hear the musical confusion
Of hounds and echo's combination

THESEUS

We will, fair queen, up to the mountain's top,
And mark the musical confusion
Of hounds and echo in conjunction.

> Note: He means the echoing of the dogs barking and also refers to Echo, a nymph in Greek mythology. Zeus loved entertaining the beautiful young nymphs on Earth. Zeus's wife, Hera, became suspicious and descended from Mt. Olympus to catch Zeus with the nymphs. Echo, in trying to defend Zeus, angered Hera. She put a spell on Echo making her able to speak only the last few words spoken to her, like an echo. Subsequently, when Echo met Narcissus and fell in love with him, she was unable to tell him how she felt and was forced to watch him fall in love with himself.

HIPPOLYTA

I was with Hercules and Cadmus once in a wood in Crete where they hunted bear with Spartan hounds. Never before did I hear such heroic howling. Not only the woods, but the skies, the fountains, everywhere around seemed to echo one big cry. I never heard such musical discord, nor such sweet thunder.

HIPPOLYTA

I was with Hercules and Cadmus once,
When in a wood of Crete they bayed the bear
With hounds of Sparta. Never did I hear
Such gallant chiding, for, besides the groves,
The skies, the fountains, every region near
Seemed all one mutual cry. I never heard
So musical a discord, such sweet thunder.

> Note: Cadmus did not hunt bear with Hercules. He was the brother of Europa and founded Thebes in Boeotia in Greek mythology. He killed a dragon which guarded a spring. When he planted the dragon's teeth, armed men grew from the soil. He set them fighting each other, the survivors formed the ancestors of the Theban nobility.
>
> Shakespeare often mixes opposites when describing things: e.g. musical discord, sweet thunder.

THESEUS

My hounds are bred from the Spartan pedigree. Large chaps, sandy coloured, heads low with ears sweeping the morning dew, bowed legs and loose throat flesh, like Greek Thessalian bulls. Slow in pursuit, but with voices like church bells, harmonising each other. A more tuneful cry was never hollered to nor cheered on with hunting horns in Crete, in Sparta, nor in Thessaly. You can judge for yourself when you hear them.

THESEUS

My hounds are bred out of the Spartan kind,
So flewed, so sanded; and their heads are hung
With ears that sweep away the morning dew;
Crook-kneed, and dew-lapped like Thessalian bulls;
Slow in pursuit, but matched in mouth like bells,
Each under each. A cry more tuneable
Was never holla'd to nor cheered with horn
In Crete, in Sparta, nor in Thessaly.
Judge when you hear.

> Note: Hunting dogs with a musical quality to their cries were much favoured, with breeds separated by the sweetness, the loudness and the deepness of their mouth (voice). A 'cry' is the collective name of a pack of hunting dogs.

THESEUS SEES THE LOVERS ASLEEP ON THE GROUND.

THESEUS

But wait, what young ladies are these?

THESEUS

But soft, what nymphs are these?

EGEUS POINTS OUT WHO EACH OF THE SLEEPERS ARE.

EGEUS

My lord, this is my daughter asleep here, and this is Lysander, this is Demetrius, this is Helena – old Nedar's daughter. I wonder why they are all here together.

EGEUS

My lord, this is my daughter here asleep;
And this, Lysander; this Demetrius is;
This Helena, old Nedar's Helena.
I wonder of their being here together.

THESEUS

No doubt they arose early to observe the rite of May, and hearing of our intentions came here to honour our pre-marriage ceremony. But tell me, Egeus, is this not the day that Hermia should announce her decision?

THESEUS

No doubt they rose up early to observe
The rite of May; and, hearing our intent,
Came here in grace of our solemnity.
But speak, Egeus; is not this the day
That Hermia should give answer of her choice?

EGEUS
It is, my lord.

EGEUS
It is, my lord.

Note: *Her decision is whether to marry her father's choice of suitor, Demetrius, or be killed for disobeying his orders.*

THESEUS
Go, tell the huntsmen to wake them with their horns.

THESEUS
Go, bid the huntsmen wake them with their horns.

EXIT ATTENDANT.

HORNS BLOW AND SHOUTS WITHIN.

LYSANDER, DEMETRIUS, HELENA AND HELENA WAKE UP.

THESEUS (CONT'D)
Good morning, friends. St. Valentine's Day is long past. Are these wood pigeons beginning to pair off only now?

THESEUS
Good morrow, friends. Saint Valentine is past;
Begin these wood-birds but to couple now?

Note: *In folklore, birds paired off for the mating season on St. Valentine's Day.*

LYSANDER IS EMBARRASSED AT BEING CAUGHT RED HANDED IN A COMPROMISING SITUATION. HE APOLOGISES.

LYSANDER
I do beg your pardon, my lord.

LYSANDER
Pardon, my lord.

THESEUS
I beg you all, stand up.

THESEUS
I pray you all, stand up.

THE LOVERS STAND UP SHEEPISHLY. THESEUS ADDRESSES THE MEN.

THESEUS (CONT'D)
I know you two are rival enemies. So how come this peaceful harmony reigns in your world?
Hatred is a long way from jealousy
To sleep near hate and fear no injury?

THESEUS
I know you two are rival enemies;
How comes this gentle concord in the world
That hatred is so far from jealousy
To sleep by hate, and fear no enmity?

LYSANDER

My lord, my reply may be bewildering, as I am still half asleep and half awake. At the moment though, I swear, I cannot truthfully tell how I came to be here. But, I think... (*he thinks*)... for I wish to only speak the truth... (*thinks*) and now I do believe it is beginning to come back to me. I came here with Hermia - (*he hesitates*) our intention was to flee Athens where we might escape the peril of Athenian law...

EGEUS

(*interrupting*) Enough, enough, my lord, you've said enough. I demand the law, the law, come down on him. They would have run away.
(*to Demetrius*) They would, Demetrius! They would have robbed us - you of your wife and me of my consent, of my consent that she should be your wife.

DEMETRIUS

My lord, sweet Helena told me of their secret flight, and their plans to come to this wood, and I in a fury followed them, sweet Helena following me out of love. But, my good lord, - I don't know by what power, but by some power it was – my love for Hermia melted like snow. The memory of it now seems like the trivial playthings of my childhood which I once doted on. And in all truth, the idol of my heart, the object and pleasure in my eye, is now only Helena. To her, my lord, I was engaged before I saw Hermia. But just like a sickness I started loathing this food. And as my health and appetite returned, I found myself wishing it, loving it, longing for a different food, and will forever more be faithful to it.

LYSANDER

My lord, I shall reply amazedly,
Half asleep, half waking; but as yet, I swear,
I cannot truly say how I came here.
But, as I think - for truly would I speak -
And now I do bethink me so it is:
I came with Hermia hither - our intent
Was to be gone from Athens where we might
Without the peril of Athenian law -

EGEUS

Enough, enough, my lord, you have enough.
I beg the law, the law, upon his head.
They would have stol'n away, they would,
  Demetrius,
Thereby to have defeated you and me -
You of your wife and me of my consent,
Of my consent that she should be your wife.

DEMETRIUS

My lord, fair Helen told me of their stealth,
Of this their purpose hither to this wood,
And I in fury hither followed them,
Fair Helena in fancy following me.
But, my good lord - I wot not by what power,
But by some power it is - my love to Hermia,
Melted as the snow, seems to me now
As the remembrance of an idle gaud
Which in my childhood I did dote upon;
And all the faith, the virtue of my heart,
The object and the pleasure of mine eye,
Is only Helena. To her, my lord,
Was I betrothed ere I saw Hermia;
But like in sickness did I loathe this food;
But, as in health come to my natural taste,
Now I do wish it, love it, long for it,
And will for evermore be true to it.

Note: He is comparing his previous love, Helena, to food he stopped liking, desiring a new different food.

THESEUS

Dear lovers, it is fortunate you met. Of this we will discuss more of later.
- Egeus, I will over-rule your wishes, for in the temple shortly, with us, these couples will be eternally joined. And now, as it is late in the morning, our proposed hunt will be postponed.
Away with us to Athens! Couples three
We'll hold a feast of great ceremony.
Come on, Hippolyta.

THESEUS

Fair lovers, you are fortunately met.
Of this discourse we more will hear anon.
Egeus, I will overbear your will;
For in the temple, by and by, with us
These couples shall eternally be knit:
And, for the morning now is something worn,
Our purposed hunting shall be set aside.
Away with us to Athens! Three and three,
We'll hold a feast in great solemnity.
Come, Hippolyta.

EXEUNT THESEUS, HIPPOLYTA, EGEUS, AND ATTENDANTS, LEAVING THE
LOVERS AND BOTTOM, WHO IS STILL ASLEEP.

DEMETRIUS

These memories seem distant and difficult to make out, like mountains so far away they look like clouds.

DEMETRIUS

These things seem small and undistinguishable,
Like far-off mountains turned into clouds.

HERMIA

It's as if I am seeing things through squinted eyes, everything seems to be in double vision.

HERMIA

Methinks I see these things with parted eye,
When everything seems double.

HELENA

Me too, I think, and Demetrius is like a jewel I have found, he's mine, yet he's not mine.

HELENA

So methinks;
And I have found Demetrius like a jewel,
Mine own, and not mine own.

DEMETRIUS

Are you sure we're awake? It seems to me we are still asleep and dreaming. Wasn't the Duke here, and didn't he ask us to follow him?

DEMETRIUS

Are you sure
That we are awake? It seems to me
That yet we sleep, we dream. Do not you think
The Duke was here and bid us follow him?

HERMIA

Yes, and my father too.

HERMIA

Yea, and my father.

HELENA

And Hippolyta.

HELENA

And Hippolyta.

LYSANDER

And he asked us to follow him to the temple.

LYSANDER

And he did bid us follow to the temple.

DEMETRIUS

Well then, we are awake. Let's follow him, and along the way we can recount our dreams.

DEMETRIUS

Why, then, we are awake. Let's follow him; And by the way let us recount our dreams.

EXEUNT ALL BUT THE SLEEPING BOTTOM.

BOTTOM AWAKES.

BOTTOM

(*waking*) When my cue comes, call me, and I'll speak. My next cue is, "Most fair Pyramus".

BOTTOM

When my cue comes, call me, and I will answer. My next is ' Most fair Pyramus'.

BOTTOM LOOKS AROUND CONFUSED.

HE CALLS TO THE OTHERS.

BOTTOM (CONT'D)

(*calling*) Hello!
Peter Quince!
Flute, the bellows mender!
Snout, the tinker!
Starveling!
On my life, they've sneaked away and left me asleep! I have had a most bizarre dream. I had a dream beyond the imagination of a man to say what the dream was. If a man tried to explain the dream he would sound like an ass. I thought I was... no man can say what. I thought I was... and I thought I had... but a man would seem a fool if he tried to say what I thought I had. No eye of man has heard, no ear of man has seen, no man's hand is able to taste, his tongue conceive or his heart describe what my dream was. It shall be called Bottom's Dream, because it has no bottom. And I will sing it in the latter part of the play, in front of the Duke. Or perhaps to make it more appropriate, I'll sing it when Thisbe dies.

BOTTOM

Heigh-ho! Peter Quince! Flute, the bellows-mender! Snout, the tinker! Starveling! God's my life, stolen hence, and left me asleep! I have had a most rare vision. I have had a dream past the wit of man to say what dream it was. Man is but an ass if he go about to expound this dream. Methought I was - there is no man can tell what. Methought I was - and methought I had - but man is but a patched fool if he will offer to say what methought I had. The eye of man hath not heard, the ear of man hath not seen, man's hand is not able to taste, his tongue to conceive, nor his heart to report, what my dream was. I will get Peter Quince to write a ballad of this dream. It shall be called Bottom's Dream, because it hath no bottom; and I will sing it in the latter end of a play, before the Duke; peradventure, to make it the more gracious, I shall sing it at her death.

Note: 'Patched fool' – jesters, clowns. The name comes from the coloured, patched outfits which jesters wore.

Act IV Scene I - Another Part Of The Wood, Later On.

EXIT BOTTOM.

ACT IV SCENE II

ATHENS. QUINCE'S HOUSE

> Note: These are comic actors who mix up their words and their grammar. They speak in prose.

ENTER QUINCE, THISBE (FLUTE) AND THE RABBLE, (SNOUT AND STARVELING).

QUINCE
Have you sent word to Bottom's house? Is (has) he come home yet?

STARVELING
He can (has) not be (been) heard of. There's no doubt he is (has been) kidnapped.

FLUTE
If he comes not, then the play is ruined. It *won't* go forward, *does* it?

QUINCE
It is not possible. There's not a man in all Athens able to *discharge* Pyramus like him.

QUINCE
Have you sent to Bottom's house? Is he come home yet?

STARVELING
He cannot be heard of. Out of doubt he is transported.

FLUTE
If he come not, then the play is marred. It goes not forward, doth it?

QUINCE
It is not possible. You have not a man in all Athens able to discharge Pyramus but he.

> Note: Throughout the play characters say 'discharge' instead of 'act' or 'play' the part

FLUTE
No, he simply has the best wit of any handyman in Athens.

QUINCE
Yes, and the best character too, and he is a complete *paramour* of a sweet voice.

FLUTE
You must say 'paragon'. A paramour is – God bless us – a thing of naughtiness.

FLUTE
No, he hath simply the best wit of any handicraft man in Athens.

QUINCE
Yea, and the best person too; and he is a very paramour for a sweet voice.

FLUTE
You must say `paragon'. A paramour is - God bless us - a thing of naught.

> Note: A paramour is a lover, a paragon is a model of excellence.

ENTER THE JOINER (SNUG).

SNUG

Men, the duke is coming from the temple, and there *is* two or three lords and ladies married. If our play had gone ahead, we would all have been rich men.

FLUTE

Oh, sweet bully Bottom! So he has lost sixpence a day for life. He would not have missed out on sixpence a day. I'll be hanged if the duke would not have given him sixpence a day for playing Pyramus, he would have deserved it. Sixpence a day for Pyramus, or nothing.

SNUG

Masters, the duke is coming from the temple, and there is two or three lords and ladies more married. If our sport had gone forward, we had all been made men.

FLUTE

O sweet bully Bottom! Thus hath he lost sixpence a day during his life; he could not have 'scaped sixpence a day. An the duke had not given him sixpence a day for playing Pyramus, I'll be hanged. He would have deserved it: sixpence a day in Pyramus, or nothing.

> Note: The sixpence would have been the pension some actors were awarded by the monarch or nobility if they had enjoyed a particular performance.

ENTER BOTTOM.

BOTTOM

Where are these men? Where are these stout fellows?

QUINCE

Bottom! Oh, most *courageous* day! Oh, most happy hour!

BOTTOM

Where are these lads? Where are these hearts?

QUINCE

Bottom! O most courageous day! O most happy hour!

> Note: Courageous is not the correct word here, it is another 'blunder'.

BOTTOM

Gentlemen, I have some amazing wonders to discourse, but don't ask me any details, for if I told you, I would not be a true Athenian. I will tell you everything, right as it happened.

QUINCE

Let us hear, sweet Bottom.

BOTTOM

Masters, I am to discourse wonders; but ask me not what; for if I tell you, I am not true Athenian. I will tell you everything, right as it fell out.

QUINCE

Let us hear, sweet Bottom.

BOTTOM

Not a word out of me. All that I will tell you is that the duke has dined. Get your costumes together, strong strings to tie your beards on, new laces for your shoes. Meet right away in the palace. Every man read through your lines, for the short and the long of it is, our play is chosen. In any case, Thisbe must have a clean dress, and don't let the man who plays the lion trim his nails, for they will protrude as the lion's claws. And most importantly, dear actors, do not eat onions or garlic, for we must utter our words with sweet breath. And I do not doubt that we shall hear them say it is sweet *comedy*. No more words Go! Get going!

BOTTOM

Not a word of me. All that I will tell you is that the duke hath dined. Get your apparel together, good strings to your beards, new ribbons to your pumps. Meet presently at the palace. Every man look o'er his part; for the short and the long is, our play is preferred. In any case, let Thisbe have clean linen; and let not him that plays the lion pare his nails, for they shall hang out for the lion's claws. And, most dear actors, eat no onions nor garlic, for we are to utter sweet breath; and I do not doubt but to hear them say it is a sweet comedy. No more words. Away! Go, away!

Note: Again, Bottom calls the play a comedy, when it is very much supposed to be a tragedy.

EXUENT.

ACT V

ATHENS

THE PALACE OF THESEUS

THIS IS THE TRUE BEGINNING OF OUR END

ACT V

ACT V SCENE I

ATHENS. THE PALACE OF THESEUS.

ENTER THESEUS, HIPPOLYTA, PHILOSTRATE, WITH LORDS AND ATTENDANTS.

HIPPOLYTA

It's strange, my Theseus, what these lovers talk of.

THESEUS

More strange than true. I'll never believe these old folktales, or these fairy stories. Lovers and madmen have such heated brains, such inventive imagination, dreaming of things cool reasoning could never comprehend. The lunatic, the lover, the poet, are all similarly imaginative. One sees more devils than the vastness of hell can hold, that is the madman. The lover, just as wild, sees Helen of Troy's beauty in the face of a gypsy. The poet's eye, in a frenzied inspiration, glances from heaven to earth, from earth to heaven, and from imagination creates images of things previously unknown, which the poet's pen turns into reality, giving them shape and form with the use of words. Strong imagination can play such tricks that if it feels some joy, it has to invent some fantastical cause for that joy.
Like in the night, frightened with some fear,
A bush becomes an imaginary bear!

HIPPOLYTA

'Tis strange, my Theseus, that these lovers speak of.

THESEUS

More strange than true. I never may believe
These antique fables, nor these fairy toys.
Lovers and madmen have such seething brains,
Such shaping fantasies, that apprehend
More than cool reason ever comprehends.
The lunatic, the lover, and the poet,
Are of imagination all compact.
One sees more devils than vast hell can hold,
That is the madman. The lover, all as frantic,
Sees Helen's beauty in a brow of Egypt.
The poet's eye, in a fine frenzy rolling,
Doth glance from heaven to earth, from earth to
  heaven;
And as imagination bodies forth
The forms of things unknown, the poet's pen
Turns them to shapes, and gives to airy nothing
A local habitation and a name.
Such tricks hath strong imagination
That if it would but apprehend some joy,
It comprehends some bringer of that joy;
Or in the night, imagining some fear,
How easy is a bush supposed a bear!

Note: 'Gypsy' – the word derived from 'gipcyan', short for Egyptian. He is saying that lovers see the beauty of Helen of Troy in any woman who comes from that part of the world. Troy was on the coast of modern day Turkey but in Shakespeare's time the location was not known.

HIPPOLYTA

But all the stories they've told of the night, and all their minds seem to be so united. Truth, rather than mere imagination, shows great consistency, however strange and fanciful it may seem.

HIPPOLYTA

But all the story of the night told over,
And all their minds transfigured so together,
More witnesseth than fancy's images,
And grows to something of great constancy;
But, howsoever, strange and admirable.

ENTER THE LOVERS – LYSANDER AND HERMIA, DEMETRIUS AND HELENA.

THESEUS

Here come the lovers, full of joy and high spirits. Happiness, dear friends, happiness and love be in your hearts with each new day!

THESEUS

Here come the lovers, full of joy and mirth.
Joy, gentle friends; joy and fresh days of love
Accompany your hearts!

LYSANDER

May even more be with you in your royal walks, your table and your bed!

LYSANDER

More than to us
Wait in your royal walks, your board, your bed!

THESEUS

Well now, what masquerades, what dances shall we have to wear away the long weary three hours between supper and our bed time? Where is the planner of festivities? What revels are planned? Is there no play to ease the boredom of a tortuous hour? Call Philostrate.

THESEUS

Come now; what masques, what dances shall we
  have
To wear away this long age of three hours
Between our after-supper and bed-time?
Where is our usual manager of mirth?
What revels are in hand? Is there no play
To ease the anguish of a torturing hour?
Call Philostrate.

PHILOSTRATE STEPS FORWARD.

PHILOSTRATE

Here, mighty Theseus.

PHILOSTRATE

Here, mighty Theseus.

THESEUS

Tell me, what entertainment have you planned for this evening? A masque? Music? How shall we overcome the tedious time without some delights?

THESEUS

Say, what abridgement have you for this evening?
What masque, what music? How shall we beguile
The lazy time, if not with some delight?

PHILOSTRATE

Here is a list of many entertainments ready for you.

PHILOSTRATE

There is a brief how many sports are ripe.

PHILOSTRATE HANDS HIM A PAPER.

PHILOSTRATE (CONT'D)
Chose which your highness wishes to see first.

THESEUS
(reading) - "The battle of the Centaurs," to be sung by an Athenian castrati to harp accompaniment. -
(stopping reading) We won't have that. That story I have told my love in praise of my cousin, Hercules.

PHILOSTRATE
Make choice of which your highness will see first.

THESEUS
[Reading.]
-"The battle with the Centaurs," to be sung
By an Athenian eunuch to the harp. -
We'll none of that. That have I told my love
In glory of my kinsman, Hercules.

Note: Castrati were male singers, castrated when young to prevent puberty and keep the high singing voice of a young boy. Eunuchs were men also castrated who kept guard over women in oriental harems. The term 'castrati' did not come about until the 18th century, long after Shakespeare's time.

Centaurs were mythical creatures, having the body and legs of a horse but the head and torso of a man. It is also the name for a tribe of renowned horsemen from Thesally (in north eastern Greece).

THESEUS (CONT'D)
(reading)
"The frenzy of the drunken Bacchanals,
tearing Orpheus apart in their rage."
(stopping reading) That is an old story, and it was played to me when I returned from conquering Thebes.

THESEUS
[Reading.]
- "The Riot of the Tipsy Bacchanals,
Tearing the Thracian singer in their rage." -
That is an old device, and it was played
When I from Thebes came last a conqueror.

Note: 'Bacchanals' – frenzied followers of the god Dionysus (Bacchus in Roman mythology). In a wild orgy they tore the poet Orpheus apart for excluding all female company after the loss of his wife, Eurydice.

'Thracian singer' – Orpheus was a renowned singer from the ancient country of Thrace in Greek mythology.

Theseus, with an Athenian army, captured Thebes. Despite this he did not allow the Athenians to occupy or loot Thebes.

THESEUS CONT'D)
(reading)
"The nine Muses mourning for the death of learning, lately deceased in poverty."
That is serious satire, sharp and critical, not suitable for a wedding ceremony.

THESEUS
[Reading.]
- "The thrice three Muses mourning for the death
Of learning, late deceased in beggary." -
That is some satire, keen and critical,
Not sorting with a nuptial ceremony.

> *Note: "Thrice three Muses mourning for the death of learning" – The Muses in mythology are the nine daughters of Zeus who preside over the arts and sciences. Shakespeare often uses the number three or multiples of it especially in mystical or magical circumstances, the number three is used often in Macbeth and was considered to have mystical powers.*
>
> *This may have been a reference to Spencer's poem "The Tears of the Muses", which bemoaned the decline in literature and learning. It is also thought to be a reference to Robert Greene, who wrote a scathing review of Shakespeare and others in his publication "A Groatsworth Of Wit" shortly before he died in poverty (beggary). Green was a highly educated (learned man), a "university wit" who believed Shakespeare was not qualified to write plays as he was a lowly grammar school educated boy.*

THESEUS

(reading)

  " A tediously short scene of young Pyramus
  and his love Thisbe." Very tragic comedy.
Comedy and tragedy! Tedious and short!
That's like hot ice, and wondrously
strange black snow. How shall we find
sense in this nonsense?

THESEUS

[Reading.]

  - "A tedious brief scene of young Pyramus
  And his love Thisbe," very tragical mirth. -
Merry and tragical! Tedious and brief!
That is hot ice and wondrous strange snow.
How shall we find the concord of this discord?

> *Note: "Wondrous strange snow". It is generally agreed that there is an error in this line as one would expect an oxymoron (two opposing terms) to follow "hot ice". Many guesses have been made as to what it should have said instead of 'strange', such as 'scorching', 'seething', 'swarthy' 'staining' etc. These all have two syllables ('strange' has one) as the line is short of one syllable, unless 'wondrous' is pronounced as three syllables.*
>
> *Important Note: The word 'black' has been added to the translation to match the look and feel of "hot ice" with 'black snow', but the word "black" must be ignored for exam and study purposes.*

PHILOSTRATE

It's a play, my lord, some ten words long,
which is as 'short' a play as any I've
known, but it is, my lord, too long by ten
words, which makes it 'tedious' - for in all
the play there is not one appropriate
word, nor one actor suited to his role. And
a 'tragedy', my noble lord, it certainly is.
For in it Pyramus kills himself, which I
must confess made my eyes water when I
saw the play rehearsed, with more tears
of loud laughter than were ever shed
before.

PHILOSTRATE

A play there is, my lord, some ten words long,
Which is as ` brief' as I have known a play;
But by ten words, my lord, it is too long,
Which makes it ` tedious'; for in all the play
There is not one word apt, one player fitted.
And ` tragical', my noble lord, it is,
For Pyramus therein doth kill himself;
Which when I saw the play rehearsed I must
  confess
Made mine eyes water; but more ` merry' tears
The passion of loud laughter never shed.

THESEUS
Who are they that perform it?

PHILOSTRATE
Manual labourers who work here in Athens, men who never laboured their minds with any art before, and who now memorise this play with their unpractised minds for your marriage.

THESEUS
Then we will hear it.

PHILOSTRATE
No, my noble lord, it's not suitable for you. I have heard it all, and it makes no sense, no sense at all in the world. Unless you can find fun in their attempts to impress you, pushing themselves to their limits of learning amidst much suffering,

THESEUS
What are they that do play it?

PHILOSTRATE
Hard-handed men that work in Athens here,
Which never laboured in their minds till now;
And now have toiled their unbreathed memories
With this same play against your nuptial.

THESEUS
And we will hear it.

PHILOSTRATE
No, my noble lord;
It is not for you. I have heard it over,
And it is nothing, nothing in the world;
Unless you can find sport in their intents,
Extremely stretched and conned with cruel pain,
To do you service.

Note: "And it is nothing". During Shakespeare's time 'nothing' was a euphemism for female genitalia. So depending how this line is delivered, it could be very condescending about the play, or just brushed off as an unimportant piece of nonsense. (A man had something between his legs, a woman had nothing – her 'nothing'). Back then it was pronounced 'nuttin' or 'nottin', depending on regional accent, with a hard 'T'.

THESEUS
I will hear the play.
Anything unsophisticated and offered with good intention can never be bad. Go, bring them in.
- And take your places, ladies.

THESEUS
I will hear that play;
For never anything can be amiss
When simpleness and duty tender it.
Go, bring them in; and take your places, ladies.

EXIT PHILOSTRATE TO GET THE ACTORS (CLOWNS).

HIPPOLYTA
I don't like to see simple folk overstretching themselves, and going down badly out of duty to us.

HIPPOLYTA
I love not to see wretchedness o'ercharged,
And duty in his service perishing.

THESEUS
My gentle sweetheart, you'll see no such thing.

THESEUS
Why, gentle sweet, you shall see no such thing.

HIPPOLYTA

He says they have no ability in this kind of thing.

THESEUS

All the kinder we are then to give them thanks for a poor performance. Our enjoyment will be in enduring the mistakes they make, and showing noble respect for the effort, not the ability, these poor creatures have planned, anxious to show their duty to us. In the past, great scholars have attempted to greet me with rehearsed welcomes, and I have seen them shake and turn pale, halting in mid sentence, losing their voice to their fears, silently failing to finish, not welcoming me at all. Trust me, sweetness, out of this silence I still realised the welcome, and in the nervousness of their fearful duty I saw as much welcome as from any unscrupled tongue of wit and audacious eloquence. Lovers and tongue-tied simpletons say more when they speak less in my opinion.

HIPPOLYTA

He says they can do nothing in this kind.

THESEUS

The kinder we, to give them thanks for nothing.
Our sport shall be to take what they mistake;
And what poor duty cannot do, noble respect
Takes it in might, not merit.
Where I have come, great clerks have purposed
To greet me with premeditated welcomes;
Where I have seen them shiver and look pale,
Make periods in the midst of sentences,
Throttle their practised accent in their fears,
And in conclusion dumbly have broke off,
Not paying me a welcome. Trust me, sweet,
Out of this silence yet I picked a welcome;
And in the modesty of fearful duty
I read as much as from the rattling tongue
Of saucy and audacious eloquence.
Love, therefore, and tongue-tied simplicity
In least speak most to my capacity.

RE-ENTER PHILOSTRATE.

PHILOSTRATE

If it so pleases your grace, the Prologue is ready.

THESEUS

Let him enter.

PHILOSTRATE

So please your grace, the Prologue is addressed.

THESEUS

Let him approach.

FLOURISH OF TRUMPETS.

ENTER QUINCE TO READ THE PROLOGUE.

PROLOGUE (QUINCE)

If we offend, then it is our intent.
  Should you think we did not come to offend,
Only with good intent. To show our art,
  That is the real beginning of our end.
Consider that we come only in spite.
  We do not come with reason to please you,
Is our true intent. All for your delight
  We are not here. So we should upset you
The actors are at hand. And, by their show
You shall know all that you're likely to know.

PROLOGUE

If we offend, it is with our good will.
  That you should think we come not to offend
But with good will. To show our simple skill,
  That is the true beginning of our end.
Consider then we come but in despite.
  We do not come as minding to content you,
Our true intent is. All for your delight
  We are not here. That you should here repent you
The actors are at hand; and, by their show
You shall know all that you are like to know.

Note: Due to bad punctuation, Quince has said the complete opposite of what he meant. He meant to say that if they caused offence, it was unintentional, they came only with the intent of showing off their simple skills. They only came to please people, not to make them sorry.

With correct punctuation (and ignoring the line breaks) it should have read, "If we offend, it is with our good will that you should think we come not to offend, but with good will to show our simple skill. That is the true beginning of our end. Consider then; we come, but in despite we do not come – as minding to content you. Our true intent is all for your delight. We are not here that you should have repent you. The actors are at hand, and by their show you shall know all that you are like to know."

Or translated – "If we offend you, it is with our best intentions that we come here not to offend you, but with the good intentions of showing off our simple skills. That is the real meaning of our aim. (the incorrect punctuation suggests they will be executed for their poor performance). Consider that we come here not in spite, we are here to entertain you. Our true intention is only for you to be delighted. We are not here for you to regret watching. The actors are ready, and by their performance you will learn everything.

THESEUS

This fellow does not understand punctuation.

THESEUS

This fellow doth not stand upon points.

LYSANDER

He's ridden his prologue like an un-tame colt, he doesn't know when to pause. A good lesson, my lord: it's not enough just to speak, but to speak correctly.

LYSANDER

He hath rid his prologue like a rough colt; he knows not the stop. A good moral, my lord: it is not enough to speak, but to speak true.

HIPPOLYTA

Indeed, he has played his prologue like a child on a recorder – it makes a sound, but it's not harmonious.

HIPPOLYTA

Indeed, he hath played on his prologue like a child on a recorder - a sound, but not in government.

Note: A recorder is a wooden musical instrument children learn.

THESEUS

His speech was like a tangled chain –
nothing wrong with each part, but the
whole of it in disorder. Who is next?

THESEUS

His speech was like a tangled chain - nothing
impaired, but all disordered. Who is next?

A TRUMPETER ENTERS, FOLLOWED BY BOTTOM AS PYRAMUS, FLUTE AS THISBE,
SNOUT AS WALL, STARVELING AS MOONSHINE AND SNUG AS LION. THEY STEP
FORWARD ONE BY ONE AS QUINCE (PROLOGUE) INTRODUCES THEM.

PROLOGUE

Gentlemen, you may wonder at this show.
But wonder on, till truth makes all things
*   clear.*
This man is Pyramus, so that you know,
And this fair lady, is Thisbe, for sure.
This man with lime and cement represents
A vile wall, that does keep these loves apart.
And through Wall's chink, pour souls, they are
*   content*
To whisper. What about let no man ask.
This man with lantern, dog and bush of thorn,
Will represent moonshine, for don't you know,
By moonshine did these lovers think no wrong
To meet at Ninus' tomb, there, there to woo.
This grisly beast, which Lion is his name,
The faithful Thisbe, meeting first that night,
Did scare away, or rather gave a fright.
And as she fled her shawl she did let fall,
Which lion, vile with bloody mouth did stain.
And soon comes Pyramus, sweet youth so tall,
And finds his faithful Thisbe's shawl there lain.
At which with blade, with bloody blameful
*   blade,*
He bravely broached his boiling bloody breast.
Then Thisbe, lying low in bushy shade,
His dagger drew, and died. For all the rest,
Let Lion, Moonshine, Wall and lovers two,
Stay here a while for to explain to you.

PROLOGUE

Gentles, perchance you wonder at this show;
*   But wonder on, till truth make all things plain.*
This man is Pyramus, if you would know;
*   This beauteous lady Thisbe is, certain.*
This man with lime and rough-cast doth present
*   Wall, that vile wall which did these lovers sunder;*
And through Wall's chink, poor souls, they are content
*   To whisper. At the which let no man wonder.*
This man with lanthorn, dog, and bush of thorn,
*   Presenteth Moonshine; for, if you will know,*
By moonshine did these lovers think no scorn
*   To meet at Ninus' tomb, there, there to woo.*
This grisly beast, which Lion hight by name,
*   The trusty Thisbe, coming first by night,*
*   Did scare away, or rather did affright;*
And as she fled her mantle she did fall,
*   Which Lion vile with bloody mouth did stain.*
Anon comes Pyramus, sweet youth and tall,
*   And finds his trusty Thisbe's mantle slain;*
Whereat with blade, with bloody blameful blade,
*   He bravely broached his boiling bloody breast;*
And Thisbe, tarrying in mulberry shade,
*   His dagger drew, and died. For all the rest,*
Let Lion, Moonshine, Wall, and lovers twain,
*   At large discourse while here they do remain.*

Note: The prologue was badly written for comic effect, the translation has largely
kept the original wording and the alliterations (words starting with the same letter)
such as 'bravely broached his boiling bloody breast' – which means stabbed himself
in the chest – to keep the feel of the original. The story is explained in Act I Scene II.

EXEUNT PROLOGUE, PYRAMUS, THISBE, LION AND MOONSHINE.

WALL REMAINS.

THESEUS

I wonder if the lion is going to speak.

DEMETRIUS

I wouldn't surprise me, my lord, if one lion can speak when so many asses do.

WALL

In this short interlude it does befall
That I, one Snout by name, will play a wall.
And such a wall as I would have you think
That had in it a hole, a gap or chink,
Through which the lovers, Pyramus and
*   Thisbe,*
Did whisper often, very secretly.
This clay, this stone, these bricks all do behold
That I am that same wall, if truth be told.
And here the hole is, right and sinister,
Through which the fearful lovers will whisper.

THESEUS

I wonder if the lion be to speak.

DEMETRIUS

No wonder, my lord. One lion may when many asses do.

WALL

In this same interlude it doth befall
That I, one Snout by name, present a wall;
And such a wall as I would have you think
That had in it a crannied hole or chink,
Through which the lovers, Pyramus and Thisbe,
Did whisper often, very secretly.
This loam, this rough-cast, and this stone, doth show
That I am that same wall; the truth is so;
And this the cranny is, right and sinister,
Through which the fearful lovers are to whisper.

WALL DEMONSTRATES BY HOLDING UP HIS HAND
AND IMITATING A HOLE.

THESEUS

Could you hope for plaster and mortar to speak any better?

THESEUS

Would you desire lime and hair to speak better?

> Note: Lime and hair were mixed together to make plaster and mortar. Theseus is being sarcastic. It is ridiculous that a wall is speaking.

DEMETRIUS

It is the wittiest partition that I ever heard speak, my lord.

DEMETRIUS

It is the wittiest partition that ever I heard discourse, my lord.

RE-ENTER PYRAMUS (BOTTOM).

THESEUS

Pyramus approaches the wall. Silence!

THESEUS

Pyramus draws near the wall. Silence!

BOTTOM GIVES AN OVERLY DRAMATIC PERFORMANCE.

PYRAMUS

Oh, grim looking night! Oh, night hue so black!

Oh, night which always is when day is not!

Oh night, oh night, alack, alack, alack,

I fear my Thisbe's promise is forgot!

And you, oh wall, oh sweet, oh lovely wall,

That stands between her father's ground and mine,

You wall, oh wall, oh sweet and lovely wall,

Show me your chink to blink through with mine eyne.

PYRAMUS

O grim-looked night! O night with hue so black!

O night which ever art when day is not!

O night, O night, alack, alack, alack,

I fear my Thisbe's promise is forgot!

And thou, O wall, O sweet, O lovely wall,

That stand'st between her father's ground and mine;

Thou wall, O wall, O sweet and lovely wall,

Show me thy chink to blink through with mine eyne.

Note: 'Eyne' - again Shakespeare uses the poetic word for eyes.

WALL HOLDS UP HIS FINGERS, IMITATING A HOLE.

PYRAMUS (CONT'D)

Thanks, courteous wall. God guard you well for this!

But what see I? No Thisbe can I see.

Oh, wicked wall, through you I see no bliss.

Cursed be your stones for so deceiving me!

PYRAMUS

Thanks, courteous wall. Jove shield thee well for this!

But what see I? No Thisbe do I see.

O wicked wall, through whom I see no bliss;

Cursed be thy stones for thus deceiving me!

THESEUS SPEAKS HIS OPINION LOUDLY.

THESEUS

The wall I think, if it's sensible, should curse back.

THESEUS

The wall, methinks, being sensible, should curse again.

BOTTOM STEPS OFF THE STAGE TO EXPLAIN, BREAKING THE GOLDEN RULE OF
NOT BREAKING THE FOURTH WALL, (INTERACTING WITH THE AUDIENCE).

PYRAMUS

(*stubbornly*) No, in fact, sir, he should not. 'Deceiving me' is Thisbe's cue. She is to enter now, and I am to spy her through the wall. You shall see, it will all fall together as I told you. Here she comes.

PYRAMUS

No, in truth, sir, he should not. `Deceiving me' is Thisbe's cue. She is to enter now, and I am to spy her through the wall. You shall see, it will fall pat as I told you. Yonder she comes.

RE-ENTER THISBE (FLUTE). BOTTOM STEPS BACK ON STAGE.

THISBE

Oh wall, so often you have heard my moans,
For parting my love Pyramus and me!
My cherry lips have often kissed your stones,
Your stones with clay and mortar joining thee.

THISBE

O wall, full often hast thou heard my moans,
For parting my fair Pyramus and me!
My cherry lips have often kissed thy stones,
Thy stones with lime and hair knit up in thee.

> Note: 'Kissed your stones' – an amusing unintentional innuendo by Thisbe.

PYRAMUS

I see a voice, now I'll go to the chink,
To spy so I can hear my Thisbe's face.
Thisbe!

PYRAMUS

I see a voice; now will I to the chink,
To spy an I can hear my Thisbe's face.
Thisbe!

> Note: He has of course mixed up his words. He cannot see a voice or hear a face.

THISBE

My love! You are my love, I think?

PYRAMUS

Think what you will, your love I do embrace,
And like Limander I am faithful still.

THISBE

My love! Thou art my love, I think?

PYRAMUS

Think what thou wilt, I am thy lover' grace;
And like Limander am I trusty still.

> Note: 'Limander' – he means Leander from Greek mythology, the lover of the priestess, Hero. He drowned swimming across the Hellespont trying to meet her. Thisbe gets 'Helen' wrong in the next line, she means Hero. When Leander drowned, Hero threw herself into the sea in grief and joined him in death.

THISBE

And I like Helen, till the fates do kill.

THISBE

And I like Helen, till the fates me kill.

> Note: Again the punctuation is wrong, it should say "And I, like Helen, (am faithful) till the fates kill me". Or more accurately it should say 'Hero' not Helen.
>
> The 'Fates' were three goddesses who determined a human's destiny, or fate as we also call it. One spun (made) the thread of life, one decided its length, and one cut it.

PYRAMUS

Shafalus was not to Procrus so true.

THISBE

Like Shafalus was to Procrus, I'm to you.

PYRAMUS

Not Shafalus to Procrus was so true.

THISBE

As Shafalus to Procrus, I to you.

> Note: 'Shafalus' should be Cephalus, and 'Procrus' should be Procris, who were married to each other. The goddess Aurora fell in love with the mortal, Cephalus, and tried to seduce him, but he rejected her, remaining faithful to his wife. But his wife, Procris, feared Cephalus had been unfaithful, and one day when he was hunting she hid in the woods to spy on him. He heard a noise and threw his spear, killing her. The story is from Ovid's 'Metamorphoses'.

PYRAMUS

Oh, kiss me through the hole in this vile wall!

PYRAMUS

O, kiss me through the hole of this vile wall!

HE PUTS HIS LIPS TO WALL'S FINGERS AND KISSES THEM.

THISBE

I kiss the wall's hole, not your lips at all.

THISBE

I kiss the wall's hole, not your lips at all.

Note: This line can be delivered full of innuendo, playing on the word 'hole'.

PYRASMUS

Can you meet at Ninny's tomb straight away?

PYRASMUS

Wilt thou at Ninny's tomb meet me straightway?

THISBE

Come life, come death, I come without delay.

THISBE

Tide life, tide death, I come without delay.

EXEUNT PYRAMUS AND THISBE.

WALL

Now, have I, Wall, my part finished so,
Now, being done, this Wall away will go.

WALL

Thus have I, Wall, my part discharged so;
And, being done, thus Wall away doth go.

EXIT WALL.

THESEUS

Now the barrier is down between the two neighbours.

THESEUS

Now is the mural down between the two neighbours.

Note: Some texts say 'mural down', some say 'moral down', and some say 'moon used'. Although Moon will appear shortly, it makes better sense of the next line if it means the wall is down.

DEMETRIUS

It's not a remedy, my lord, when walls secretly hear everything.

DEMETRIUS

No remedy, my lord, when walls are so wilful to hear without warning.

Note: He is effectively saying, 'walls have ears', which means a wall is no barrier to someone else overhearing.

HIPPOLYTA

This is the silliest stuff that I ever heard.

HIPPOLYTA

This is the silliest stuff that ever I heard.

THESEUS

Even the best of these kind of things are without substance, the same as the worst, if we have to imagine how good it would be if they could act.

THESEUS

The best in this kind are but shadows; and the worst are no worse, if imagination amend them.

HIPPOLYTA

You'd have to use your imagination then, not theirs.

HIPPOLYTA

It must be your imagination then, and not theirs.

THESEUS

If we imagine they are as good as they imagine they are, then they are all excellent actors. Here come two noble beasts, a man and a lion.

THESEUS

If we imagine no worse of them than they of themselves, they may pass for excellent men. Here come two noble beasts in, a man and a lion.

> Note: This is probably Shakespeare making a sly comment about some fellow actors.
>
> Some texts amend the words "a man and a lion" to "a moon and a lion" because the Moon comes on next with the Lion, but a Moon is hardly a noble beast.

RE-ENTER LION AND MOONSHINE.

LION

You, ladies, you whose gentle hearts do fear
The smallest monstrous mouse that creeps the floor,
May now perhaps both quake and tremble here,
When rough lion in wildest rage does roar.
So know that I am Snug the joiner come
As cruel lion, and nor a lion's mum.
For if as lion I should come in wrath
Into this place, my life would have no worth.

LION

You, ladies, you whose gentle hearts do fear
The smallest monstrous mouse that creeps on floor,
May now perchance both quake and tremble here,
When lion rough in wildest rage doth roar.
Then know that I as Snug the joiner am
A lion fell, nor else no lion's dam;
For if I should as lion come in strife
Into this place, 'twere pity on my life.

> Note: 'A lion fell' is a cruel lion, and a 'lion's dam' is the mother of a lion. He has mixed up his wording – he is saying he is a lion, (when he means he is not) and nor is he a lion's dam (a lion's mother) when he means a lioness.

THESEUS

A very gentle beast, and with a good conscience.

THESEUS

A very gentle beast, and of good conscience.

DEMETRIUS

The very best at beastly acting, my lord, that ever I saw.

DEMETRIUS

The very best at a beast, my lord, that e'er I saw.

LYSANDER This lion has the courage of a fox.	**LYSANDER** This lion is a very fox for his valour.
THESEUS True, and the caution of a goose.	**THESEUS** True; and a goose for his discretion.

Note: When Theseus says the goose line after Lysander's line, it is based on the saying, "Discretion is the better part of valour" – it is better to avoid a dangerous situation than confront it. He follows the word 'valour' with 'discretion'

DEMETRIUS Not so, my lord, for his courage cannot overcome his caution, but a fox can overcome a goose.	**DEMETRIUS** Not so, my lord; for his valour cannot carry his discretion, and the fox carries the goose.
THESEUS Neither, I'm sure, can his caution overcome his courage, because a goose cannot overcome a fox. It's all good. Leave it to him to sort out, and let's hear the moon.	**THESEUS** His discretion, I am sure, cannot carry his valour; for the goose carries not the fox. It is well. Leave it to his discretion, and let us listen to the moon.

MOONSHINE STEPS FORWARD ONTO THE STAGE.

MOONSHINE This lantern represents the horned crescent moon...	**MOONSHINE** This lanthorn doth the horned moon present -

Note: 'Lanthorn' – an old term for lantern, when horns were used to make them.

HE HOLDS UP HIS LANTERN.

THE AUDIENCE HECKLES HIM.

DEMETRIUS He should have worn the horns on his head, like a cuckold.	**DEMETRIUS** He should have worn the horns on his head.

Note: In folklore, if a man's wife was unfaithful to him he would grow horns.

THESEUS He is a full moon, not a crescent, so his horns are invisible.	**THESEUS** He is no crescent, and his horns are invisible within the circumference.

MOONSHINE REPLIES TO THE COMMENTS.

MOONSHINE

(stubborn) This *lantern* represents the horned moon. Myself, I am the man in the moon it would seem.

THESEUS

This is a bigger error than all the rest. The man should be inside the lantern. How else could he be the man 'in' the moon?

DEMETRIUS

He dare not go there because of the candle, you can see, the wick is already smoking in disgust.

Note: To snuff a candle is to extinguish it or trim the wick when the candles starts smoking. The phrase "in snuff" was based on a saying "to take something in snuff", meaning, to be offended at something, one would sniff one's nose, like taking snuff (powered tobacco sniffed up the nose).

HIPPOLYTA

I am tired of this moon. I wish he would change!

THESEUS

It appears by the dimness of his courage, that he is waning. But, then again, out of courtesy, and politeness, we must endure him.

Note: Again punning on the word 'discretion' from earlier.

LYSANDER

Go ahead, Moon.

MOONSHINE

(stubbornly again) All I have to say is to tell you that the lantern is the moon. I am the man in the moon, this thorn bush is my thorn bush, and this dog is my dog.

DEMETRIUS

Well, all of these should be in the lantern then, because these are in the moon. But silence, here comes Thisbe.

MOONSHINE

This lanthorn doth the horned moon present;
Myself the man i'th' moon do seem to be.

THESEUS

This is the greatest error of all the rest; the man should be put into the lanthorn. How is it else the man i'th' moon?

DEMETRIUS

He dares not come there for the candle; for, you see, it is already in snuff.

HIPPOLYTA

I am weary of this moon. Would he would change!

THESEUS

It appears, by his small light of discretion, that he is in the wane; but yet, in courtesy, in all reason, we must stay the time.

LYSANDER

Proceed, Moon.

MOONSHINE

All that I have to say is to tell you that the lanthorn is the moon; I the man i'th' moon, this thorn-bush my thorn-bush, and this dog my dog.

DEMETRIUS

Why, all these should be in the lanthorn; for all these are in the moon. But silence; here comes Thisbe.

RE-ENTER THISBE (FLUTE, WEARING A MASK TO LOOK LIKE A WOMAN AND HIDE HIS BEARD).

THISBE
This place is Ninny's old tomb.
(*she looks around*) But where is my love?

THISBE
This is old Ninny's tomb. Where is my love?

LION
(*roaring*) ROOOOOAR!

LION
[*Roaring.*] O!

THISBE RUNS OFF, DROPPING HER SHAWL AS SHE RUNS.

DEMETRIUS
Well roared, Lion!

DEMETRIUS
Well roared, Lion.

THESEUS
Well run, Thisbe!

THESEUS
Well run, Thisbe.

HIPPOLYTA
Well shone, Moon. Truly, the moon shines very gracefully.

HIPPOLYTA
Well shone, Moon. Truly, the moon shines with a good grace.

THE LION TEARS AT THISBE'S SHAWL, LIKE A CAT WITH A MOUSE, STAINING IT WITH BLOOD AND THEN EXITS.

NOW MOONSHINE STANDS ALONE WAITING FOR PYRAMUS.

THESEUS
Well moused, Lion!

THESEUS
Well moused, Lion.

DEMETRIUS
And then came Pyramus.

DEMETRIUS
And then came Pyramus.

LYSANDER
And so the lion vanished.

LYSANDER
And so the lion vanished,

> Note: Reiterating that the lion is not very brave.

RE-ENTER PYRAMUS AS IF HE'D ALMOST MISSED HIS CUE.

PYRAMUS

Sweet Moon, I thank you for your sunny beams,

I thank you, Moon, for shining now so bright,

For by your gracious, golden, glittering gleams,

I trust to take in trusty Thisbe's sight.

PYRAMUS

Sweet Moon, I thank thee for thy sunny beams;

I thank thee, Moon, for shining now so bright;

For by thy gracious, golden, glittering gleams,

I trust to take of truest Thisbe sight.

> Note: The forced alliterations, (words all starting with the same letter) and a 'sunny' moon.

HE SEES THISBE'S SHAWL LYING ON THE GROUND.

PYRAMUS (CONT'D)

But wait, oh damn!

But look, poor man,

What dreadful grief is here?

Eyes, do you see?

How can it be?

Oh, dearest love! Oh dear!

Your shawl is tore,

And stained with gore!

Oh come, you Furies cruel!

Oh, Fates, come on,

Cut thread and yarn,

Quell, crush, conclude and kill!

PYRAMUS

But stay, O spite!

But mark, poor knight,

What dreadful dole is here?

Eyes, do you see?

How can it be?

O dainty duck! O dear!

Thy mantle good,

What, stained with blood!

Approach, ye Furies fell!

O Fates, come, come,

Cut thread and thrum,

Quail, crush, conclude, and quell!

> Note: 'Furies fell' – the Furies were three Greek goddesses who pronounced curses on the guilty and inflicted famines and plagues. 'Fell' is used here in its lesser used meaning of evil, cruel, deadly, as in the expression 'One fell swoop'.
>
> 'Fates' – the Fates were the three Greek goddesses who preside over the births and deaths of humans. They determined a human's destiny, or fate as we also call it. One spun (made) the thread of life, one decided its length, and one cut it.

THESEUS

(*sarcastic*) This outburst of emotion would almost make a man feel sad - providing a dear friend had just died.

THESEUS

This passion, and the death of a dear friend, would go near to make a man look sad.

> Note: 'Passion' – used by Shakespeare to describe any strong emotion.

HIPPOLYTA

A curse on my heart, but I do pity the man.

HIPPOLYTA

Beshrew my heart, but I pity the man.

PYRAMUS

Oh why, oh nature, have you lions made?
Since lion vile has deflowered my dear?
Who is – no, no – who was the fairest maid
That lived, that loved, that liked, that looked
 with cheer.
   Come, tears, and blind,
   Out, sword, and wound,
The breast of Pyramus.
  Ay, that left breast,
  Where heart does rest.
Like this I die, thus, thus.

PYRAMUS

O wherefore, Nature, didst thou lions frame,
 Since lion vile hath here deflowered my dear?
Which is - no, no - which was the fairest dame
 That lived, that loved, that liked, that looked with
cheer.
   Come, tears, confound;
   Out, sword, and wound
 The pap of Pyramus.
  Ay, that left pap,
  Where heart doth hop.
 Thus die I, thus, thus, thus.

> Note: 'Deflowered' – cutting a flower in its bloom. It also means death taking her virginity, which Shakespeare refers to more fully in Romeo and Juliet, "I'll to my wedding bed, and death, not Romeo, take my maidenhead!".

PYRAMUS STABS HIMSELF REPEATEDLY.

PYRAMUS (CONT'D)
  Now I am dead,
  Now I have fled.
My soul is in the sky.
  Tongue, loose your light.
  Moon, take your flight...
(he pauses, waiting for Moonshine to leave)

PYRAMUS
  Now am I dead,
  Now am I fled;
My soul is in the sky.
  Tongue, loose thy light;
  Moon, take thy flight.

> Note: Again he mixes up his words. The moon should loose its light, and his tongue (probably meaning his speech and therefore breath) should take flight. In other words, he breathes his last.

EXIT MOONSHINE, HE HAD NOT BEEN EXPECTING TO LEAVE, BUT INSTEAD TO
DOUSE HIS LIGHT, SO HE IS TAKEN BY SURPRISE.

PYRAMUS (CONT'D)
Now I die, die, die, die, die.

PYRAMUS
Now die, die, die, die, die.

PYRAMUS DIES DRAMTICALLY.

DEMETRIUS

Not a die, only an ace for him. For he is one of a kind.

DEMETRIUS

No die, but an ace for him; for he is but one.

Note: 'Die' – a dice, a cube with six numbers represented by dots, the single dot being called an 'ace'. In Shakespeare's time, 'die' was also slang for 'orgasm'. So the line could be delivered in a number of ways.

LYSANDER

Less than an ace, man. He's dead. He's nothing.

LYSANDER

Less than an ace, man; for he is dead; he is nothing.

Note: 'Nothing' had the double meaning of a woman's genitalia.

THESEUS

With the help of a surgeon he might still recover and prove an 'ass'.

THESEUS

With the help of a surgeon he might yet recover, and prove an ass.

Note: Punning 'ace' with 'ass'.

HIPPOLYTA

How come Moonshine has gone before Thisbe comes back to find her lover?

HIPPOLYTA

How chance Moonshine is gone before Thisbe comes back and finds her lover?

THESEUS

She'll find him by starlight. Here she comes – and her passionate speech will end the play.

THESEUS

She will find him by starlight. Here she comes; and her passion ends the play.

RE-ENTER THISBE.

HIPPOLYTA

I hope she doesn't make it a long one, not for a Pyramus such as this. I hope she will be brief.

HIPPOLYTA

Methinks she should not use a long one for such a Pyramus. I hope she will be brief.

DEMETRIUS

There's nothing between whether Pyramus or Thisbe is the better actor - he for being a man, God forgive us, or her, God bless us, for being a woman.

DEMETRIUS

A mote will turn the balance, which Pyramus, which Thisbe, is the better - he for a man, God warrant us; she for a woman, God bless us.

Note: He is saying Pyramus is not much of a man, being weak, and Thisbe is not much of a woman (being played by a man).

LYSANDER

She has spotted him already with those sweet eyes.

DEMETRIUS

And so she speaks, see...

LYSANDER

She hath spied him already with those sweet eyes.

DEMETRIUS

And thus she means, videlicet:

Note: 'Videlicet' is Latin, short for 'Videre licet' – 'videre' means to see, 'licet' means it is permissible. More commonly shortened to 'viz' or 'to wit" or more simply 'namely'.

THISBE

Asleep my love?
What, dead my dove?
Oh, Pyramus, arise!
Speak, speak. Quite dumb?
Dead, dead? A tomb
Must cover your sweet eyes.

THISBE

Asleep, my love?
What, dead, my dove?
O Pyramus, arise!
Speak, speak. Quite dumb?
Dead, dead? A tomb
Must cover thy sweet eyes.:

SHE NOW DESCRIBES HIM MOST ABSURDLY.

THISBE (CONT'D)

These lily lips,
This cherry nose,
These yellow cowslip cheeks,
Are gone, are gone.
Lovers will moan,
His eyes were green as leeks.

THISBE

These lily lips,
This cherry nose,
These yellow cowslip cheeks,
Are gone, are gone;
Lovers, make moan;
His eyes were green as leeks.

Note: She is mixing everything up, it should be cherry lips, not cherry nose. Cowslips are yellow flowers, not the colour of cheeks at all. Leeks are long stemmed onions.

THISBE (CONT'D)

Oh, Sisters Three,
Come, come to me,
With hands as pale as milk.
Put in my guts,
Since you've made cuts
With shears his thread of silk.
Tongue not a word.
Come, trusty sword,
Come, blade, my breast to dwell.

THISBE

O Sisters Three,
Come, come to me,
With hands as pale as milk;
Lay them in gore,
Since you have shore
With shears his thread of silk.
Tongue, not a word.
Come, trusty sword;
Come, blade, my breast imbrue:

Note: 'Sisters Three' – the three Fates who determine human destiny (fate), one spins the thread of silk, one measures the thread, and one cuts the thread determining the lifespan of a person.

137

THISBE STABS HERSELF.

THISBE (CONT'D)	THISBE
(dying)	*And farewell, friends.*
And farewell, friends,	*Thus Thisbe ends.*
Here Thisbe ends.	*Adieu, adieu, adieu.*
Farewell, farewell, farewell.	

THISBE DIES.

THESEUS	THESEUS
Moonshine and Lion are left to bury the dead.	Moonshine and Lion are left to bury the dead.
DEMETRIUS	DEMETRIUS
Yes, and Wall too.	Ay, and Wall too.

HEARING THIS, BOTTOM GETS UP FROM PLAYING DEAD AND ADDRESSES THEM.

BOTTOM	BOTTOM
(to audience) No, I assure you. The wall is down that separated their fathers. Would you like to see the epilogue, or hear a burlesque dance from two of our actors?	[*Starting up.*] No, I assure you; the wall is down that parted their fathers. Will it please you to see the epilogue, or to hear a Bergomask dance between two of our company?

> Note: Again he mixes up 'see' and 'hear'. 'Bergomask dance' is a burlesque dance from Bergamo in Italy.

THESEUS	THESEUS
No epilogue, I beg you, your play needs no excuses. Never make excuses when all the actors are dead, no one needs to be blamed. If the man who wrote it had played Pyramus and hanged himself with Thisbe's garter belt, it would have been a fine tragedy indeed. And so it is, truly, and very finely acted. But come, your Burlesque dance. Forget your epilogue.	No epilogue, I pray you; for your play needs no excuse. Never excuse; for when the players are all dead there need none to be blamed. Marry, if he that writ it had played Pyramus and hanged himself in Thisbe's garter, it would have been a fine tragedy. And so it is, truly; and very notably discharged. But come, your Bergomask; let your epilogue alone.

> Note: 'Discharged' – acted.
>
> *There is no mention of who dances. The only stage directions we have is, "a dance". It is probable that Bottom has mistaken a Bergomask dance for a masked dance because of the name (and the spelling here may be a clue). Nor is there any mention of music, it is up to each individual production how they interpret the dance.*

THE ACTORS DANCE AS A DISTANT BELL CHIMES TWELVE.

THEN EXEUNT THISBE, PYRAMUS, PROLOGUE, MOONSHINE, LION AND WALL.

THESEUS (CONT'D)	THESEUS
The iron voice of midnight has tolled twelve. Lovers, to bed, it's almost time for the fairies. I fear we shall oversleep tomorrow morning as much as we have overstayed the lateness of the hour tonight. This dreadfully dull play has speeded up the passing of the slow hours of night. Sweet friends, to bed. *For two weeks we will hold ceremonies* *In nightly revels and new jollities.*	The iron tongue of midnight hath told twelve. Lovers, to bed; 'tis almost fairy time. I fear we shall outsleep the coming morn, As much as we this night have overwatched. This palpable-gross play hath well beguiled The heavy gait of night. Sweet friends, to bed. *A fortnight hold we this solemnity* *In nightly revels and new jollity.*

Note: Fairies only come out at night.

EXUENT.

ENTER PUCK WITH A BROOM TO SWEEP UP AFTER THE CELEBRATIONS.

PUCK	PUCK
Now the hungry lion roars, * And the wolf howls at the moon,* *Whilst the weary ploughman snores,* * At the heavy tasks he's done.* *Now the burnt-out logs do glow,* * Whilst the screech-owl, screeches loud,* *Makes a wretch that lies in woe* * In memory of a shroud.*	*Now the hungry lion roars,* * And the wolf behowls the moon;* *Whilst the heavy ploughman snores,* * All with weary task foredone.* *Now the wasted brands do glow,* * Whilst the screech-owl, screeching loud,* *Puts the wretch that lies in woe* * In remembrance of a shroud.*

Note: 'Screech-owl' – the owl shrieking was an omen of someone dying. As when Lady Macbeth says, "It was the owl that shrieked, the fatal bellman, which gives the stern'st goodnight". 'The bellman' because when someone died the church bells were rung so that everyone who heard them could pray for the poor departed's soul. How they were rung determined whether a man or a woman had died, so the prayers could be adjusted to suit.

"Wretch that lies in woe" – a poverty stricken woman lying on her sickbed.

'Shroud' - People were buried in a 'shroud' – a sheet sewn around the body.

PUCK (CONT'D)

Now it is the time of night
  That the graves, all open wide,
Every grave lets out a sprite,
  To the churchyard paths to glide.
And we fairies that do run
  Beside Hecate's triple team
From the coming of the sun,
  Following darkness like a dream,
Are all merry. Not a mouse
  Shall disturb this hallowed house.
I am sent with this here broom,
To sweep the dust out of the room.

PUCK

Now it is the time of night
  That the graves, all gaping wide,
Every one lets forth his sprite,
  In the church-way paths to glide.
And we fairies, that do run
  By the triple Hecate's team
From the presence of the sun,
  Following darkness like a dream,
Now are frolic. Not a mouse
  Shall disturb this hallowed house.
I am sent with broom before,
To sweep the dust behind the door.

Note: 'Sprite' – an elf or a fairy.

'Hecate' – the goddess of dark places, also the Queen Witch in Macbeth.

'Triple team' – the team of dragons which pulled Hecate's chariot. Triple is relating to the three forms Hecate takes. Luna in heaven, Diana on earth, and Proserpina in Hell. The three forms are known as 'diva triformis'. 'Diva' literally means 'goddess' in Latin. The word didn't adopt the meaning of lead singer in opera until the late 19th century and much more recently to describe an awkward actress or singer.

ENTER THE KING AND QUEEN OF THE FAIRIES, (OBERON AND TITANIA), WITH THEIR TRAIN OF ATTENDANT FAIRIES.

OBERON

(to his Fairies)
Through the house give glimmering light,
  By the dying, drowsy fire.
Every elf and fairy sprite
  Lightly hop like bird on briar,
Sing this ditty, after me,
And dance along so flowingly.

OBERON

Through the house give glimmering light,
  By the dead and drowsy fire;
Every elf and fairy sprite
  Hop as light as bird from briar,
And this ditty, after me,
Sing and dance it trippingly.

TITANIA

Commit your song to memory,
Every word and melody.
Hand in hand, with fairy grace,
We will sing and bless this place.

TITANIA

First, rehearse your song by rote,
To each word a warbling note;
Hand in hand, with fairy grace,
Will we sing, and bless this place.

OBERON TAKES THE LEAD IN A SONG AND DANCE.

OBERON

Now, until the break of day,
Through this house each fairy stray.
To the bridal bed head we,
Which by us shall blessed be.
And the children they create
Always shall be fortunate.
So shall all the couples three
Ever true and loving be.
And the birthmarks nature brings
Shall not be on their offspring.
Nor a mole, harelip or scar,
Nor mark of omens such as are
Hated on a new baby,
Shall not on their children be.
With these drops of morning dew,
Every fairy make his way,
Each and every bedroom bless
With sweet peace in this palace,
And every owner of it blessed
Shall ever lie safe at rest.
Dance away, do not stay,
Meet me all by break of day.

OBERON

Now, until the break of day,
Through this house each fairy stray.
To the best bride-bed will we,
Which by us shall blessed be;
And the issue there create
Ever shall be fortunate.
So shall all the couples three
Ever true in loving be;
And the blots of Nature's hand
Shall not in their issue stand.
Never mole, harelip, nor scar,
Nor mark prodigious, such as are
Despised in nativity,
Shall upon their children be.
With this field-dew consecrate
Every fairy take his gait,
And each several chamber bless
Through this palace with sweet peace;
And the owner of it blest,
Ever shall in safety rest.
Trip away; make no stay;
Meet me all by break of day.

EXEUNT OBERON, TITANIA AND HER ATTENDANTS, LEAVING ONLY PUCK.

PUCK

If we spirits have offended.
Think of this, and all is mended:
That you have just slumbered here
While these visions did appear.
And this weak and feeble theme,
Is no more than a simple dream.
Gentle folk, don't reprimand.
With your pardon, we will mend.
And, as I am, an honest Puck,
And if we have outstayed our luck,
To escape the scornful hiss
We'll amend what is amiss,
Or else Puck a liar call.
So, good night unto you all.
Give me your hand, if we're still friends,
And Robin shall now make amends.

PUCK

If we shadows have offended,
Think but this, and all is mended:
That you have but slumbered here
While these visions did appear.
And this weak and idle theme,
No more yielding but a dream,
Gentles, do not reprehend.
If you pardon, we will mend.
And, as I am an honest Puck,
If we have unearned luck
Now to 'scape the serpent's tongue
We will make amends ere long;
Else the Puck a liar call.
So, good night unto you all.
Give me your hands, if we be friends,
And Robin shall restore amends.

EXIT PUCK.

THE END

Made in the USA
Las Vegas, NV
05 May 2023

71648372R00079